## As she spoke, Angel drew nearer to Gabe.

She was so close that he could feel each breath she took as her chest rose, brushing against his. When she exhaled, he felt her breath along his skin.

His gut tightened in response as he struggled to hold himself in check.

Gabe wanted to believe her. Wanted so badly just to take her into his arms and not fear the ramifications and consequences that were waiting for them just beyond the night.

But there *would* be ramifications and there *would* be consequences.

Gabe gave it one more try. "I need to find the light, Angel."

"It's right here," she whispered to him, rising on her toes, leaving her soft lips mere inches from his mouth.

Gabe could feel himself weakening. "Oh, damn, Angel, you could break a saint."

"I don't want a saint," Angel told him, her eyes never leaving his. "I want you."

Dear Reader,

Here we are, back in Forever, Texas. This time we're visiting Alma's brother, Gabe. Gabe is trying to deal with the sting of being dumped by a woman who felt she could do "better," and by "better" she meant finding someone wealthier. Alma, in an effort to get Gabe to come around, gets the sheriff to offer him a temporary position as a fill-in deputy. Gabe accepts, but there's not much to do in a small town like Forever—that is, if you don't count saving a beautiful woman's life by pulling her out of a car tottering on the brink of a ledge before it goes over—or bursts into flame (which it does, seconds after he rescues her). There's a slight hitch with the rescue. The woman doesn't know how she got there—or who she is. Impulsively, Gabe names her "Angel" because she looks like one to him (and because it's nearly Christmas).

With nothing but time on his hands, Gabe takes Angel on as his private project, trying to help her remember who she is. But as the days go by, both Gabe and Angel grow more and more reluctant to unearth her past, especially since they are growing so close to one another in the present. Still, nothing goes smoothly, and someone from Angel's past is looking for her—and he's not looking for a happy reunion.

As always, I thank you for reading, and I hope you enjoy this latest stroll through Forever. From the bottom of my heart, I wish you someone to love who loves you back.

Happy holidays!

Love,

Marie

# A Forever Christmas

## MARIE FERRARELLA

**HARLEQUIN®**
entertain, enrich, inspire™

Recycling programs
for this product may
not exist in your area.

ISBN-13: 978-0-373-75430-4

A FOREVER CHRISTMAS

Copyright © 2012 by Marie Rydzynski-Ferrarella

www.Harlequin.com

**Printed in U.S.A.**

# ABOUT THE AUTHOR

Marie Ferrarella, a *USA TODAY* bestselling and RITA® Award-winning author, has written more than two hundred books for Silhouette and Harlequin Books, some under the name of Marie Nicole. Her romances are beloved by fans worldwide. Visit her website at www.marieferrarella.com.

To
Stella Bagwell,
My Go-To Person
For All Things Western.
With Love And Thanks

# Prologue

It was the rain that was ultimately responsible.

The rain and fear.

In their own unique way, they were both blinding. The rain came down in sheets, demanding that she pull over, or at the very least drive more slowly.

The sky was close to being as dark as midnight, despite the fact that it was in the middle of the day. But there was nowhere for her to pull over, no town, no gas station. Nothing.

Nothing but exposed space.

And she couldn't risk being exposed. Even in this storm.

She didn't know if she was still even in Texas anymore.

All she knew was that she had to keep going, had to put as many miles between her and Jake as she could. There had been murder in his eyes the very last time she'd seen him.

Her murder.

He was coming for her. She could *feel* it.

She'd raced to her car, soaked before she'd ever reached it. Once inside, her hand shaking so badly it was hard to put the key into the ignition, it took her three tries to get it to turn over. Tearing away from the house, she put her foot all the way down on the gas pedal and drove as fast as she could.

Just drove. The destination didn't matter. She had to save herself.

It was her own fault.

She shouldn't have come back. She should have known he'd be watching the house, waiting for her to show up.

Jake.

The man who was the reason why she'd taken off to begin with. Why she'd changed her name, changed her appearance, changed her life. Changed everything just to get away from him.

And she had.

But when she'd learned, by accident, of her mother's death, she couldn't stay away from the funeral. Her heart ached too much not to say goodbye one last time.

She should have realized that his obsession would have had him watching the cemetery, watching the house. She'd thought she was careful, waiting for everyone to leave before she'd paused at the cemetery. Before she'd slipped into the house. She wanted to get the album of pictures her mother had kept. Pictures from a happier time. That, and her mother's locket, those were the only two things she'd wanted—almost *needed*—to see her through this awful period.

Securing them would have only taken a few minutes. In and out. But even just a few minutes were too many.

He'd been watching for her.

Waiting.

And the moment she was in the house, he'd closed in. If that floorboard hadn't squeaked when it had…

But it had and she'd bolted after throwing the jewelry box at him, hitting him squarely in the face. Bolted even as he heaped a barrage of curses at her through his bloodied lips. Curses that were drowned out by the whine of the bullet that tore by her head.

Missing her by inches.

Her heart hammering so hard she was sure it would burst, clutching the album in her arms and the locket chain woven through her fingers, she had thrown herself into her car and drove. Drove like the devil was after her.

Because he was.

She had no idea how long she'd been driving. Time and space all merged into one formless entity. Her gas tank had been full when she'd begun and now the needle was shivering around Empty.

She kept driving.

She hadn't seen his headlights—or any lights at all— in her rearview mirror for a while now, but that didn't mean he wasn't there. She knew Jake, knew how obsessed, how focused, he could be. His superiors thought of it as his dedication. They didn't know the man beneath the facade. Only she had been exposed to him. Jake would think nothing of turning off his lights and driving without them even in this storm if it meant being able to catch her off guard.

She was tired. Frightened and tired. Maybe death

*was* the answer. If she had been the one who'd died instead of her mother...

No, damn it, she wouldn't give him this final triumph over her, she wouldn't, she thought angrily. She wouldn't let him steal her life from her.

She—

The tree came out of nowhere. It was far too close for her to avoid even if she swerved to the right. She swerved anyway.

She could hear the high-pitched sound coming from her tires. The car was fishtailing, spinning out of control. She vaguely remembered something about driving into the spin even as everything else told her to turn the wheel in the opposite direction.

A scream tore from her lips a second before she hit something. The tree? Something else?

There was no time to identify it. The impact had her head hitting the steering wheel. Trying to raise her head, she blinked several times before she saw the edge of the ravine yawning before her.

And then the darkness mercifully swallowed her up even as another scream tore from her throat.

## Chapter One

The rain was finally subsiding after coming down in buckets all night.

For a while there, it had been a toss-up between using his 4x4 or debating using a canoe to get back to town this morning. Gabriel Rodriguez shook his head as he laughed shortly to himself. It figured that he'd wind up facing this deluge just when he finally decided to drop by to visit his father on the family ranch. What with everything going on in his life lately—or not going on, he thought ruefully—he'd come up with one excuse after another for not taking his father up on the invitation.

His father, Miguel Rodriguez, wasn't the type to shout or make demands. Rather, the father of six merely nodded his head and accepted whatever excuse he'd given him. That was the way the man had always been. And his soft-spoken approach had always been far more effective than shouting or giving angry ultimatums. Everyone always came around sooner than later. Though he was quick to deny it, Miguel Rodriguez knew just how to wield guilt as if it were a finely honed rapier in his hand.

The old man always got the results he was after, too,

Gabe thought. They all complied, he and his five siblings. Some a little faster than others—Alma could really dig in when she wanted to—but no one was ever immune to their father's sad brown eyes or quiet demeanor for long. The man had a very easygoing personality, unlike Miguel Jr.—Mike to his friends—who had a highly volatile one.

Mike liked to call it being passionate, but whatever term was given to it, Miguel Jr. was definitely explosive whereas Miguel Sr. was not.

"Senior" also got what he wanted far more often than "Junior" ever did.

Given the monotony of the scenery around him, Gabe's mind drifted as he drove to town and his relatively new job as deputy to Rick Santiago's sheriff.

He hadn't meant to stay as long as he had last night. Initially, he'd planned on leaving by nine, but things hadn't quite worked out that way.

Dinner had been good, the conversation even better, and somehow the time had just managed to slip away. Suddenly it was way past nine and his father was telling him that his old bedroom was still right where he'd left it—upstairs, down the hall—if he wanted to stay the night rather than taking on the elements.

By then it was raining so hard, it was as if someone had ripped open the sky.

So he'd stayed.

Besides, there was really nothing pressing in town that required him being there by dawn's early light. Forever, Texas, was one of those sparsely populated towns that really needed law enforcement officers only to settle verbal disputes that sometimes got too heated and testy. On occasion, the sheriff or any of his three deputies might be called upon to rescue the town drunk from himself—or from his less-than-contented wife who, all things considered, was the dangerous one of the two.

He'd lost track of time because he actually enjoyed his father's company, and he also knew the real reason behind the recurring frequent invitations to come for dinner. His father—like his sister, Alma—was very worried about him.

Worried because, for once in his life, he'd taken a breakup really hard. Usually he was the one doing the breaking up, or orchestrating things so that the woman he was involved with was pushed to break up with him. He did the latter to spare the woman's pride.

But this, this breakup—or, more accurately, this *dumping*—had hit him like the proverbial ton of bricks. Erica, the woman he'd come to believe that he was going to marry, had abruptly declared she'd found someone else "better suited" for her via a popular dating site— as if finding a husband-to-be was the same as shopping for a dress.

That was when he'd discovered that Erica had actually drawn up a "checklist" of traits—and possessions—that her future husband had to have.

As it turned out, the woman of his dreams turned out to be money hungry.

Looking back, he had to admit, if only to himself, that there'd been signs that Erica was more of a gold digger than the sweet, loving partner he thought she was. She was a woman who knew what she wanted out of life, and what she wanted, first and foremost, was a husband who could give her those things. *All* those things.

He, as a rancher, very obviously did not fit the bill.

He supposed that made him rather naive because he'd assumed that *that* was what love was for: to fill in the gaps.

But in Erica's case, he'd thought wrong.

"You can do better, Gabe," Alma had insisted fiercely when she'd discovered that he was no longer with Erica. "A lot better."

He'd smiled and nodded at the youngest member of his family, pretending to shrug off the breakup, but deep down being rejected like that had really bothered him.

Or perhaps, he reconsidered, not so deep down because obviously Alma had seen right through his act. Acting on her firm belief that keeping busy was the best way to forget about a painful situation, she'd casually mentioned that Larry, Sheriff Rick Santiago's third deputy, had to suddenly leave town for Fort Worth because of an urgent family matter that required his presence. That left his position temporarily vacant.

Then Alma had reminded him about all those times, when they were kids, that they'd played sheriff and cattle rustlers. Knowing that Alma had the ability of going on forever, he'd nodded, barely remembering what she was talking about.

Before he knew it, that casual, noncommittal nod turned into a job offer from Rick. He'd made it clear that the job would only be temporary. At which point Alma had piped up and said it *was* temporary—unless Larry decided not to come back.

Gabe's first reaction was to laugh and decline. But the words never rose to his lips. Instead, he turned the idea over in his head. He'd really been feeling restless ever since the breakup and this seemed like a good stopgap solution.

Who knew, maybe he'd even discover that he liked the work, liked the uniform and what it represented. And, quite truthfully, he had nothing to lose. So he'd shrugged good-naturedly and said to Rick, "Sure, if you think I'd make a good one."

Rick had smiled at him and rather than offer platitudes or say something that lacked sincerity, the sheriff had said to him, "That's what we're going to find out, isn't it?"

And then he and the sheriff had shaken hands on it.

The first couple of days on the job, Alma had stuck to him like glue, explaining absolutely everything until he began to believe his sister thought that he was six years old and incapable of understanding anything unless broken down to the simplest terms and shortest words.

On the third day, he'd just about had his fill. But before he could say as much to Alma, Rick had given her a look that succinctly and silently put the senior deputy in her place. After that, whenever she began to explain something to him, she'd stop herself, murmur, "You'll get the hang of it, Gabe," and went back to doing whatever she'd been doing.

Now, after almost four weeks, Gabe had to admit it was an interesting change of pace from being a rancher. Certainly less physically tiring. There'd been times when he'd thought about getting his own spread, but his father still needed help with the ranch now and then. Besides, that ranch technically belonged to all of them. His father had seen to that.

Around the time when they'd lost their mother, all six of them had joined forces, taking any job they could, to help their father pay off all the medical bills that had accumulated. They'd also raised money to keep the bank from taking away the ranch because their father had fallen behind in payments.

Paying off the bills was a point of honor for Miguel Rodriguez, so they had all pitched in together, pooled their resources and their money. They did everything and anything until the bills were paid off and their father was back on good terms with the bank.

That was when Miguel Sr. had them all accompany him to the bank. He'd been very mysterious about why he wanted them there, not really saying anything by way of an explanation until they were all assembled in the bank president's office. That was when he told them that he was having the title on the deed changed so that it included all their names under the word *Owner*.

Stunned, they'd tried to argue him out of it, but their father had been adamant about it, refusing to change his mind. So now they were all proud joint owners of the ranch where they had grown up. And although no one said as much to their father, as far as they were all concerned, the ranch still belonged to him. Rafe, Mike and Ray still lived on the ranch and worked it while the rest of them lent a hand whenever they were needed.

But Alma worked predominantly as a deputy and Eli

had his own spread to tend to, so that cut down on the number of "hands" his father could tap into.

Which was why he'd hesitated when Alma had initially suggested his taking Larry's place.

"It's only going to be temporary. C'mon, what've you got lose?" she'd urged in that way of hers that got people to come around no matter what it was she was pushing.

So he'd said all right, and before he knew it, he was holding his right hand up and swearing his allegiance to both the state and the town, promising to do the best job he could, "So help me, God."

And just like that, he, Gabriel Rodriguez, was a U.S. deputy sheriff.

So far, he liked it. But he had to admit, the job was far from exciting.

The rain had all but stopped. That was when he first saw it. Saw the car that appeared to be tottering on the edge of the ravine. It looked like something straight out of an action movie—and not a very good one at that.

Except that this was real.

All *too* real.

The closer he came to the scene, the worse it appeared to him.

He would have said that it looked as if someone had run the vehicle off the road—if there'd actually been a discernible road to begin with. But whether by design or accident, the end result was that the vehicle was precariously positioned on the edge of the ravine. It gave every indication of being on the verge of going over if there was so much as the slightest breeze to give it a push.

He had no idea how it had managed to withstand

the forces of the rain. In his opinion, it had rained hard enough to send the sedan plummeting into the ravine.

He supposed the fact that it hadn't came under the heading of a miracle. He would need another one if there was anyone inside that sedan who needed rescuing.

Gabe hoped the supply of miracles hadn't suddenly run dry.

He'd been a deputy sheriff for less than four weeks, but he'd been a man a great deal longer than that. And as a man, he reacted a certain way.

Basic instincts, literally honed at his father's knee, had him acting almost automatically, without needing to stop to think anything through. Seeing someone in danger, his immediate reaction was to try to help, not to "go and get help."

Gabe brought his weather-beaten 4x4 to a dead stop less than a foot away from the precariously perched sedan.

From what he could make out through the clouded windows, there *was* someone inside the car.

He caught his breath. Every second counted. The smallest wrong movement on either that person's part— or his own—and the car was going to be history. As would be the person inside.

Moving carefully around the vehicle in a wide semi-circle, Gabe assessed the situation, confirming there was only one person inside the car. A woman. And she wasn't moving.

Was she in shock, or—

Gabe pressed his lips together, contemplating his

next move. He wanted to call out, to ask the woman if she was all right, but that might startle her. Much as he wanted reassurance that she was alive, he didn't want to risk her making any sudden moves that could throw off the car's fragile equilibrium.

The most logical thing was for him to drag the woman out of the car, but that had an extremely risky downside to it.

What he needed to do, Gabe decided, was to drag the car away from the edge and back onto solid ground again with all four tires firmly planted on a flat surface.

*Easier said than done.*

Gabriel pushed his hand through his hair. He had to find a way to hook up her car and his 4x4 so that he could pull the sedan away from the edge of the ravine with a minimum of risk.

He thought of calling Mick, the town's best mechanic. The fact that Mick was also the *only* mechanic in town didn't in any way affect the fact that the man could perform miracles with vehicles of all sizes and shapes. Taking out his cell phone, Gabe looked uncertainly at the teetering sedan.

How long had it been like that? More to the point, how much longer could it *stay* that way?

But even as he pressed one of the preprogrammed numbers on his keypad, he didn't know if he had enough time to wait for Mick to get here.

What if the rain started up again, full force?

He glanced down at the screen and saw that he had only half the number of bars that he usually did. The storm was probably responsible for that.

A gravelly voice answered on the other end. Rather than a formal greeting, the man said, "Yeah?"

"Mick, it's Gabe Rodriguez."

At hearing the name, Mick's voice softened just a touch. "What can I do for you, *Deputy?*" Mick asked, putting special emphasis on Gabe's new title.

"You can get yourself out here about ten miles out of town, by Lazarus Ravine. I've got a car all set to go over the edge and I need a tow."

"Yours?"

"No—"

"Belong to anyone you know?"

"No—" Again, he didn't get time to finish.

Mick's approach to life was very cut-and-dried. "Then what's the problem?"

"There's someone in it." As he spoke, he looked into the sedan again. The woman hadn't moved. Maybe that was just as well. If she came to—if she was *able* to come to—she might panic. One wrong move might prove fatal, not to mention her last. "I don't think she's conscious from what I can see. But if I try to get her out—"

"She'd fall into the ravine. I get it. Sit tight. I'm on my way," the man promised. And with that, the connection was broken.

*Sit tight.* Ordinarily that would have sounded like good advice. Gabe thought. But in all good conscience, he couldn't take it, not when a woman's life quite literally hung in the balance.

He was torn.

Anything he could do might result in making it

worse, he reasoned. Still, he didn't feel comfortable about just sitting here and waiting for Mick. A lot could happen in that short amount of time.

Right about now, hauling the town drunk into one of the jail cells to sleep it off was beginning to sound like an enviable alternative to this.

He continued to stare at the sedan.

He hadn't heard any sounds coming from the woman inside so he still didn't even know if she was dead or alive, but went with the latter.

Feeling somewhat anxious, Gabe returned to his 4x4 and began to look through both the cab and the cargo area, searching for either a really thick, strong length of rope or, better yet, a chain that he could use to hook up to the victim's car.

He finally found a length of chain all but hidden at the back of the cargo area. It was buried underneath a large pile of his belongings, which had been there since he'd moved into town a few months ago. He'd yet to sort through them and decide whether to bring them to his new living quarters, leave them at the ranch in case he decided to move back or just throw them out.

A triumphant, strongly voiced "Yes!" escaped his lips when he saw the chain. Pulling it out of the truck bed, he vaguely remembered that he'd used the chain to help remove a rotting tree stump on Eli's property. That had to be over six months ago, he realized.

"That'll teach Alma to stop nagging me about never putting anything away," he muttered under his breath, even though there was no one around to overhear him.

At the time, he'd secured the chain around the stump

and then anchored it to the back of his vehicle. Once he was sure it would hold, he slowly coaxed the stump out of the ground by driving away in almost slow motion.

It had taken close to half an hour and three separate tries, but finally the stump had come out of the ground. Most of its roots were still attached.

"Here's hoping we have the same luck here," he said to himself. Gabe looked into the sedan one more time. The woman inside still hadn't moved. How long had she been like that?

He was wasting time, wondering instead of doing, he admonished himself.

Working as fast as he could, Gabe secured one end of the chain to the rear bumper of the woman's car and the other end to his truck's front bumper. Offering up bits and pieces of a prayer his mother had insisted that all her children learn by the time they were old enough to talk, Gabe got in behind the wheel of his truck, threw it into Reverse and ever so slowly backed up.

He never took his eyes off the sedan and its still passenger.

The ground was exceedingly wet after the storm and traction not what it could have been, but of the two vehicles, his, fortunately, was the heavier one. Otherwise, he might have found himself sliding *toward* the one in jeopardy, not away from it.

He held his breath as his truck continued to slowly move away from the edge of the ravine.

Little by little, inch by inch, the sedan began to tilt toward him, away from the ledge, until finally he managed to get all four of the vehicle's wheels on the ground. Still in Reverse, he got the sedan far enough away from the edge of the ravine so that it no longer was in any danger of tumbling into it.

The second he got the other vehicle securely on flat ground, Gabe quickly turned off his engine and jumped out of the truck. Rushing over to the banged-up sedan, he found that the doors on both sides were jammed shut. Rather than attempt to wrestle with them, trying to pry one of them free, he took out the firearm that the sheriff had issued to him.

Turning it around so that the butt of the weapon was facing the window, he struck at the windshield as hard as he could. Two attempts later, the glass finally cracked. Under the forceful pressure of his hand, the small, spidery cracks began to spread out. As they did so, they weakened the glass enough so that when he swung the hilt of his weapon against it, the windshield finally shattered. Parts of it fell into the car.

Which left the rest for him to deal with. Moving quickly, Gabe removed chunks of the glass until he'd managed to clear a sufficiently large enough opening for him to snake through. He made it into the passenger seat, glass fragments clinging to his hair, casting small rainbows.

The woman was still strapped into her seat. There was blood over her right eye thanks to the head wound directly above it.

She was blonde and probably not more than about twenty-six, he judged. Her eyes were closed and for a moment he thought she was dead. Feeling her neck for a pulse, he wasn't sure if he detected any, or if what he felt faintly throbbing was merely the pulse within his own fingers.

He moved the blonde gently back so that she was in a more accessible sitting position. Gabe put his head against her chest, straining to detect even the faintest of heartbeats.

He didn't hear anything.

But just as he was straightening up, he thought he felt the slightest brush of material against his cheek. Stunned, he stared at her chest intently. That was when he saw it. Just the smallest hint of movement.

She was breathing.

The woman was still alive!

His pulse began to race and he grinned.

She was still alive.

## Chapter Two

Gabriel was torn between leaving the woman where she was until help arrived and trying to get her out of her totaled vehicle.

Weighing pros and cons, he was leaning toward the former since the ground was wet and he had no idea what sort of internal injuries she'd sustained. Since he had no medical training, he was afraid that moving her, if he unintentionally did it the wrong way, might make things worse for the blonde.

But the silent debate ended abruptly when he became aware of the very strong smell of gasoline. It was coming from her car, never a good thing considering the kind of damages the vehicle had sustained.

Staying in the wrecked vehicle was definitely not a safe choice for either one of them. Gabriel shifted, trying first one door, then the other, hoping that at least one of them was more pliable from the inside of the sedan than from the outside.

But they weren't. Neither door gave an inch, nor gave any indications that they could be moved if enough pressure was applied.

They remained sealed even when he attempted to kick his way out.

The force he'd exerted reverberated all the way up his leg to his thigh. The door still didn't budge.

Since the doors appeared to be permanently sealed, he thought his next best bet was the front windshield. He'd already crawled in through the windshield to reach the unconscious woman, but that had been at a price. He'd gotten half a dozen or more cuts along his arms and torso for his trouble. Using this route to get out meant he had to do some more cleaning up. The woman was already bleeding from her scalp. He didn't want to add to her injuries if he could help it.

Bracing himself on the seat, Gabriel raised both of his legs up as high as he could, then kicked against the windshield as hard as he was able.

It wasn't enough.

He did it again.

And again.

With each kick, a little more of the windshield shattered and drops of glass rained down on either the hood or directly into the car. Before he'd gotten started, he'd covered up the blonde with his jacket as best he could, trying to protect her from the falling glass.

Taking his jacket back now, he wrapped it around his arm, and then swung his arm in a giant sweeping motion, clearing away as much of the broken glass fragments as he could. He wanted to be able to get her out, onto the hood, with as little of the jagged edges grabbing on to her as possible.

Gabe was well aware that the maneuver would have

been a great deal easier if there was someone outside the vehicle to hand her off to. But he was fighting against the clock. Who knew how much more of a safety zone he had left to work with? He had the uneasy feeling that the car could blow up at any moment and he needed to get them both out of there and in the clear before that happened.

Besides, taking a closer look, he saw that she was still bleeding from her temple. He needed to get the blonde into town and to the doctor.

It occurred to Gabe, as he struggled to get the unconscious woman through the opening he'd created, that a year ago there would have been no doctor to take her to. At least, none in Forever and none around for a fifty-mile radius. Any medical emergency had to be handled in Pine Ridge, which boasted of a hospital within the town limits. Before Dan Davenport had arrived, Forever had been without a doctor for the past thirty years.

And now they had one.

Forever wasn't exactly a shining beacon of progress, but they were getting there, little by little, Gabe thought. He supposed that baby steps were better than no steps at all.

Despite the fact that it was cold and the woman he was struggling to get out of the car was little more than just a slip of a thing, Gabe found himself working up a sweat. There just wasn't all that much space to successfully maneuver in.

Pausing to catch his breath, he rubbed the perspiration from his forehead with the side of his forearm before it fell into his eyes.

"Okay now," he muttered, positioning his hands where he knew she would have protested had she only been conscious, he squared his shoulders and shoved, "one last big push."

Exhaling the breath he'd been holding, he experienced a surge of triumph. She was out! Time for him to be the same.

Gabriel scrambled out of the mangled death trap himself.

A small spark seemed to materialize out of nowhere. The sudden gleam reflected in the side mirror caught his eye. Gabriel instantly reacted even before the actual image even registered in his mind.

His feet hitting the ground, he grabbed the blonde up in his arms and raced to his truck. Pushing her into the passenger seat, he had just enough time to jump in behind the wheel and throw the vehicle into Reverse. His foot urgently pressing the accelerator all the way down to the floor, he put as much distance as humanly possible between his truck and the totaled sedan.

He did it just in time. The spark had multiplied, giving birth to flames that grew instantly larger and larger, as well as more insistent. By the time he'd gotten three hundred feet between his truck and the sedan, the latter blew up.

He sat in the cab of his truck, staring in disbelief at what very easily could have been his funeral pyre—or at the very least, hers.

Tension riddled his six-foot-two frame, even as he closed his eyes and exhaled.

"Guess we both just used up our share of luck for the

next fifty years," he speculated quietly, addressing his words to the unconscious blonde in the seat beside him.

His nerves badly rattled, Gabriel took a few deep breaths to try to steady his nerves. It would take more than that, but he kept at it, knowing he needed to get a grip on his emotions. People would be asking questions and he was vaguely aware that he had to put this all down in a report.

It started to rain again.

Nature was putting out the fire, he thought absently, unable to look away.

He was so completely focused on what had just happened that he remained almost totally oblivious to his surroundings for at least a couple of minutes. By the time he saw the other two vehicles, they were all but on top of him.

The weather-battered tow truck led the way. Mick had come, just as he'd promised.

The second vehicle was a Jeep. The official markings on its sides proclaimed it to belong to the sheriff's department. As they approached, the Jeep suddenly picked up speed and wound up reaching him first.

Barely coming to a complete stop, the deputy inside the vehicle jumped out. Alma hit the ground running at her top speed.

Reaching the truck, she cried out breathlessly, "Are you all right?"

"Yeah, I'm fine," Gabriel told her, dismissing himself. "But she's not." And then his mind suddenly backtracked, remembering. His only call had been to Mick.

He'd stated the problem. He had *not* asked for reinforcement. "What are you doing here?" he asked.

"Having a heart attack," Alma retorted. She nodded toward the scruffy mechanic in the worn sheepskin jacket and faded overalls.

"Mick called the sheriff's office as soon as he hung up with you. I picked up the call," she added needlessly. Satisfied that her brother had no mortal wounds, she seemed to relax a little. For the first time, she took note of the woman slumped beside him on the passenger seat. "What happened to her?"

Gabe shrugged, his wide shoulders reinforcing his answer. "Damned if I know. I was driving into town when I spotted her car." He nodded in the general direction of the ravine. "It was tottering on the edge, two wheels in the air and set to drop like a stone at the slightest shift in weight."

"And she didn't say how that happened?"

Gabe shook his head. "She was unconscious when I got there." His eyes shifted toward Mick. The mechanic was now standing behind Alma. With the sedan burned, there was nothing for the man to tow or fix. "Sorry I got you out here for no reason, Mick," he apologized.

Mick rubbed the ever-present graying stubble along his chin as he looked back at what was left of the sedan. "Oh, I dunno. Might take it back to the shop, anyway, and do me a little detective work on the remains. Figure out why it burned," he explained, adding, "Things are a might slow right now. Could use the diversion." He paused and peered closer into the cab of Gabe's truck. "You don't need a tow in or nuthin', do you?"

With a pleased smile, Gabe sat up and affectionately patted the dashboard. "She handled herself just like the trouper she is, Mick."

Mick beamed with satisfaction, like a parent whose child had remembered all his lines in the school play. "That's 'cause she had a good mechanic," Mick pointed out matter-of-factly. Then he nodded at the woman whose car was now a charred heap and asked, "What are you gonna do about her?"

Alma already had her cell out. "I'll call ahead to the doc, tell him we've got an emergency coming in." She looked at her brother. "Two emergencies," she corrected. When Gabe raised one quizzical eyebrow, she said, "Have him check out both of you."

"I'm fine," Gabriel told her firmly. He absolutely hated being fussed over, especially when the person doing the fussing was a doctor.

With a sigh, Alma shifted the cell phone to her other hand. Leaning in, she ran the tips of two of her fingers along his bare arm. Holding up "Exhibit A" for Gabe's perusal, she said, "Not from where I'm standing. You've got cuts on both your arms, big brother. You're seeing the doctor." There was no room for argument in her tone.

Gabe tried, anyway. "But—"

Alma leveled a pointed, silencing look at him. "You're seeing the doctor, Gabe," she repeated with deadly conviction, "even if I have to beat you senseless to do it."

He laughed shortly. That was Alma. If sweet talk

didn't work, she instantly turned to verbal threats, which in turn bore fruit if necessary.

"Comforting," he cracked.

"I wasn't trying to be comforting," Alma informed him crisply. "I was just trying to keep you from bleeding to death. Don't want or need you preying on my conscience, Gabriel."

Gabe gave up arguing the point directly and resorted to shifting the focus of the conversation.

"I'm more concerned about her," Gabe said. He took out a handkerchief and wiped away some of the blood on the blonde's forehead.

The handkerchief fell from his fingers when he heard the woman moan.

It was the first actual sign of life he'd gotten from her. "You're okay," he said to the blonde with feeling. "You're with friends."

"Friends she ain't met yet," Mick, who'd been silent for the most part, now quipped before walking away to take a closer look at what remained of the car.

It was still raining. Not nearly as badly as it had been earlier, but sufficiently enough to put out what there still was of the fire. Plumes of smoke twisted and turned in the air before fading off to become part of the atmosphere.

Alma looked at Gabe uncertainly. She knew the way he thought, knew the way all her brothers thought. Each and every one of them believed he was indestructible. It was a common family failing.

"You sure you're okay to drive?" she pressed. "Because I could—"

Gabe knew where this was going and quickly cut his sister off.

"I'm okay," he assured her, then after a beat, added in a quieter voice, "Thanks for asking."

For a second, Alma was speechless, then flashed her brother a tight smile. Stepping back from the truck, she told him, "I'll drive behind you to make sure you don't suddenly need something."

Gabe didn't see himself needing anything, suddenly or otherwise, but he knew there was no point in arguing. All he could do was just restate his position. "I'm okay, but suit yourself."

"Thanks for your permission," Alma said dryly, though he could tell she was doing her best to cover up her fear of losing him.

Gabe grinned for the first time since Alma had come on the scene. "Don't mention it."

Alma waved a dismissive hand at him as she walked away.

Mick was busy hooking up his tow truck to what was left of the woman's charred sedan and Alma was getting back into her Jeep while making the call to Dan's office to let the doctor know that he had an emergency patient coming in. Neither one of them saw the woman in Gabe's truck suddenly sit up as he started the vehicle again.

"No!"

The single word tore from her lips. There was terror in her eyes and she gave every indication that she was going to jump out of the truck's cab—or at least try to. Surprised, Gabe quickly grabbed her by the arm with his free hand, pulling her back inside the vehicle and into her seat.

"I wouldn't recommend that," he told her.

The fear in her eyes remained. If anything, it grew even larger.

"Who are you?" the blonde cried breathlessly. She appeared completely disoriented.

"Gabriel Rodriguez." Since he knew the name would mean nothing to her, he added, "I'm the guy who pulled you out of your car and kept you from becoming a piece of charcoal."

Her expression didn't change. It was as if his words weren't even registering. Nonetheless, Gabe paused, giving her a minute as he waited for her response.

But the woman said nothing.

"Okay," he coaxed as he continued driving toward Forever, "your turn."

The world, both inside the moving vehicle and outside of it, was spinning faster and faster, making it impossible for her to focus. Moreover, she couldn't seem to manage to pull her thoughts together. Couldn't get passed the heavy hand of fear that was all but smothering her, pushing her deep into the seat she was sitting on.

"My turn?" she echoed. What did that mean, her turn? Her turn to do what, go where?

"Yes, your turn," he repeated. Then, because she looked no clearer on the concept than she had a second ago, he elaborated. "I told you my name. Now you tell me yours."

Her name.

The two words echoed in her brain, encountering only emptiness.

The silence stretched until it was a long, thin thread, leading nowhere. Finally, just before he repeated his question again, she said in a small voice, hardly above a whisper, "I can't."

She was afraid, he thought. She didn't trust him. He could accept that. Considering what she had just gone through, there was little wonder at her reaction.

He did his best to reassure her.

"Look, I'm a deputy sheriff," he told her, adding, "I can protect you. You can tell me your name."

Suddenly very weary, she strained very, very hard, searching, waiting for something to come to her.

Anything. A scrap.

But nothing did.

Not so much as a fragment, not the smallest of pieces occurred to her.

Nothing but darkness and formless shadows.

The terror in her sky-blue eyes grew as she turned them on him. She wet her lips before speaking. It didn't help. The dryness went down several layers, into her very soul.

"No, I can't," she repeated hoarsely.

This job would take more patience than he'd initially thought. Patience and skill. It certainly was different from what he'd imagined.

He owed Alma an apology, Gabe decided, for saying that being a deputy in this county was a very slow-paced, boring job.

So much for *that,* he thought sarcastically.

"We'll protect you," he told the woman again, but he could see that no matter how he said it, it made no difference to her. Her expression—confused, frightened—didn't change. Obviously his assurance had no effect on her. He peeled back another layer, approaching the problem from another direction. "And why can't you tell me your name?"

"Because," she began, then stopped herself. She could feel bars going up, safeguards rising out of nowhere, intended to keep this man out.

Why?

Was she like that with everyone, or was it just him? And was he really a good Samaritan who'd been passing by, at the right time, in the right place, just in time to "rescue" her, or was that a story he'd made up to lull her into a false sense of security?

And why would he do that?

Exactly who was he to her?

More importantly, who was *she* to her?

She felt suddenly hollow and incredibly empty with no clue how to remedy either.

"Because—" Her voice broke. Taking a deep breath, she pushed on again and this time finished her sentence. "Because I don't know who I am." Anger and frustration echoing in her voice.

She was kidding, right? Gabe thought. When she said nothing more, he pressed, "You're serious? This isn't some kind of a joke you're playing?"

When she made no answer, he spared her a glance, thinking to coax the answer from her, or at least search her face for a clue as to whether or not she was actually telling the truth—although, when it came to reading people, Joe Lone Wolf, the sheriff's other deputy and coincidentally also his brother-in-law, was a lot better at that than he was.

One glance at the blonde told Gabriel he wasn't about to coax anything out of her, or discern anything from her expression, either.

She was unconscious again.

## Chapter Three

His first thought was to stop driving and just pull over to the side. But then what? It wasn't as if he knew what to do—he didn't. And neither, he was fairly certain, did his sister. As for the mechanic who was behind them towing in the burned remains of the woman's sedan, if it didn't have an engine in it, Mick had no clue what to do or not do, so he'd be less than no help in this situation, either.

No, the best thing that he could do for this mystery woman was just to drive and get her to the doctor as fast as possible. At least Dan could cauterize her wound and patch it up. And maybe the former New York surgeon knew how to tell whether or not the blonde was telling the truth when she claimed not to know who she was.

It began to rain heavier.

Squaring his shoulders, Gabe pressed down on the accelerator and sped up. Having lived here all his life, he knew the terrain in and around Forever like the back of his hand. If need be, he could drive to town with his eyes shut, so the threat of more obscuring rain had absolutely no effect on him.

But, in an odd sort of way, the woman in the passenger seat did.

What was it like not knowing who you were?

If this woman was actually telling the truth and not just being evasive for some reason, he imagined that it had to be pretty damn scary, not knowing your own name. When life got tough, a person was supposed to be able to rely on himself or herself. But if you didn't even know who you were, how were you supposed to depend on yourself?

"Who are you?" Gabe asked softly as he spared the unconscious blonde a long glance. "Is there someone somewhere worrying about you? Wondering why you didn't come home, or call, or even…?"

His voice trailed off as more and more questions popped up in his head. Questions that would have to go unanswered for the time being. With any luck, most of them would be addressed when the woman regained her consciousness again.

For all he knew, there might be a missing-persons file on her waiting for them by the time he got into the office.

"I know I'd be looking for you if you were mine," he murmured under his breath.

Even disheveled, with her light blond hair plastered against her face, he could see that she was beautiful. Genuinely beautiful, not one of those women whose looks came out of jars and containers and the clever application of makeup.

He put the windshield wipers on high and drove a tad faster.

WITH HIS WINTER COAT thrown carelessly over his shoulders to impede the bone-freezing weather from getting to him, Dr. Dan Davenport stood outside his single-story clinic, waiting for the patient that Alma had called him about. The November chill was creeping into his bones when he finally saw the three-vehicle caravan approaching.

*Finally,* he thought, moving to meet them.

"Slow day at the clinic, Doc?" Gabe called out as he jumped out of the cab of his truck and rounded the hood, crossing over to the passenger's side.

"Everyone's healthy at the same time for a change," Dan answered.

Which, as far as he was concerned, was a good thing. It balanced out the days when it seemed as if his waiting room was stuffed with patients from first light to way beyond the last.

Reaching the vehicle, the doctor opened the passenger door before Gabriel had a chance to. He frowned as he peered into the truck, then looked at Gabe. "She hasn't regained consciousness yet?"

"No, she did," Gabriel said. He was unaware that he had elbowed the doctor out of his way to get to the woman, but Alma noticed as she came to join them. In the background, Mick was driving on to his garage, the barbecued sedan in tow behind him. "For about two, three minutes," Gabe qualified, "and then she lost consciousness again."

"Did she tell you her name while she was still conscious?" Alma asked.

Gabe backed out of the truck's cab slowly, gently

holding the woman he'd just lifted out of the seat. Earlier, when he ran carrying her in his arms, he'd been much too intent on making sure they survived to notice just how light she actually felt in his arms.

It was as if she barely weighed anything at all.

The trite saying "light as a feather" seemed rather appropriate in this case. Light as an unconscious feather, he added ruefully.

"No," Gabe said aloud, following the doctor back into the clinic. "She doesn't know her name."

The answer stopped Alma in her tracks. "Doesn't know her name?" she repeated, puzzled. "What do you mean, she doesn't know her name?"

"Just what I said," Gabe told her. He didn't turn around, but continued to follow Dan once they were inside the clinic. "She said she didn't know her name. Looked a little panicked when she said it, too."

Dan led them straight to the only examination room that was attached to another small room in the rear of the building. The latter doubled as a makeshift overnight recovery room where people who Dan performed minor surgeries on stayed the night to recuperate.

In New York, where he'd done his residency, Dan had been a very promising up-and-coming surgeon. But because of a promise he'd made to his late younger brother, also a surgeon, he'd come out to Forever to take his place. His brother had firmly believed in "giving back." After a while, Dan began to understand what his brother had meant. And so, what was supposed to have been just a short-term mission turned into his life's work.

Dan was surprised to discover that he'd never felt better about himself than he had this past year.

"You think she's telling the truth?" Alma asked her brother skeptically. She looked down at the unconscious woman as Gabe placed her on the exam table, per Dan's instructions.

It was Dan, not Gabe, who answered.

"Very possibly," the doctor allowed. "She took a pretty good blow to the head," he judged, sizing up the head wound on her forehead just above her right eye. "That can really shake a person up."

"But she's going to snap out of it, right?" Gabe asked. "It'll all come back to her, won't it? I mean, she'll remember her name and why she wound up tottering on that ledge the way she did. Right?"

Dan raised his shoulders in a wide shrug. "I don't know," he said honestly. "Maybe. Maybe not. I've heard of some amnesia cases going on for years, with the patient not any closer to getting any answers than they'd been at the very beginning. With other patients, it's only a matter of a few hours. There's really no telling how long it could actually take."

*Years?*

The single word echoed in his head as Gabe looked at the still, unconscious face. The very idea sent a chill down his spine. He couldn't picture enduring something like that himself. It was like a virtual prison sentence that extended to eternity.

Gabe turned to the doctor. "So what do we do?" he asked.

Dan could only give him the most general of terms.

Everyone was different and healed at their own pace—if they healed at all.

"We go slow," he counseled. "Give her some space and make sure that she doesn't feel pressured, just secure. Sometimes, the harder you try, the less progress you actually make." Shrugging out of his coat and switching to a clean lab jacket, Dan paused to wash his hands. "Now, if you two don't mind, I need you to leave me alone with my patient so I can attend to her wounds."

As Gabe reluctantly began to leave, Dan raised his voice and called after him. "Stick around, though. After I get done, I think it would be a good idea to take this woman to the hospital in Pine Ridge and get a CT scan of her head to make sure that everything's all right." Drying his hands, he looked from one deputy to the other. "I'll need one of you to drive her over there."

Gabe surprised Alma by speaking up first. "I'll do it.

"Who do you think she is?" Gabe asked her once they were in the waiting room. For now, the room appeared to be empty.

"I haven't the faintest idea," Alma told him. "We could try going through the county's recent missing-persons files posted on the internet. If there's no match for her, I can widen the search. With any luck, she'll probably get her memory back before then."

"What makes you say that?" he asked, curious.

"Well, I'd say that having a car blow up a couple of seconds after you escape out of it can be pretty traumatizing. That kind of thing can cause temporary amnesia because the person isn't able to deal with it right when it happened. It's the brain's way of protecting you," she added by way of an explanation. Alma abruptly stopped talking when she saw the quizzical way her brother was staring at her. "What?"

Gabe shook his head, clearly impressed. "I never realized you knew so much."

"I'm not quite sure whether to be flattered that you're impressed, or insulted because you thought I was dumb."

"Not dumb," he quickly corrected, and then lost some steam as he added, "just, well, my little sister."

"And consequently, dumb," she concluded. Alma gave him a reproving look. "You might recall that I took college courses online and that I *do* have a degree in criminology."

Going to college online had been the only way she could have gotten her degree and still worked to help pay off her father's huge pile of bills. Both causes were equally important to her.

"Must've slipped my mind," Gabe confessed, then focused on what she'd said. "So you really think she'll remember who she is?"

"If you mean is she suddenly going to pop up like toast and have total recall, probably not right away," Alma judged, "but in time, I think it will all come back to her."

"And in the meantime?" he asked, sounding rather eager.

"Don't get ahead of yourself, Gabe," Alma cautioned. "Just take one step at a time."

"You're the one who always said to be prepared," he reminded her. "What if she never remembers who she is? Or it takes her a long time before she does? What if no one's out there looking for her, or they didn't have enough sense to file a missing-persons report? What'll we do with her until then?" he asked. "There's no motel or boardinghouse to put her up in."

"Forever's a nice, friendly town," Alma pointed out and then went on to assure her brother that, "We'll think of something. But first things first. The doc said to have her checked out at the Pine Ridge hospital once he's finished. So we need to get her there." Ever the protective one, especially now that her mother was gone, Alma said, "I know you volunteered, but if you're having second thoughts, I can take her to the hospital."

That might mean that she wouldn't be back until morning. A newlywed, his sister belonged home at night.

Gabe laughed, turning down her offer. "And have that lawyer husband of yours with his hundred-dollar words come looking for me? No, thanks. I'll take the mystery woman to the hospital."

Alma's protective streak instantly rose to defend her husband. "He only uses those words when he's in court. You're family."

"And I'd like to keep on being family," Gabe informed her. "So I'll be the one taking her to Pine Ridge." When he saw Alma smiling at him knowingly, it was his turn to ask, "What?"

"You're really taken with her, aren't you?" she asked, pleased.

Gabe stared at her. In his opinion, his sister had just made one hell of a leap—and it led to nowhere. "She's the first person I ever rescued from a car that was about to go over the side of a ravine, and then it burst into flames, so if that's what you mean by 'taken,' then, yeah, I guess I'm 'taken' with her."

His eyes narrowed as he reminded her of an important point. "You were the one who thought that I should get involved in this—and by 'this,'" he clarified, knowing how prone Alma could be to misinterpreting things if it suited her purposes, "I mean the sheriff's department."

"I did and I still do," Alma was quick to agree. "I'm just surprised, that's all. You don't usually pay attention to anything I say."

"That's because, up until now," Gabe deadpanned, "you weren't saying anything really worthwhile listening to or going along with."

"According to you," she qualified.

"According to me," he agreed with the most unreadable expression he could muster.

Alma glanced at her watch and rose to her feet.

"I'm going to go and update Rick about what's going on with our mystery woman and then I'll be back. If you decide that you've changed your mind about going to Pine Ridge—"

He cut her off. "I won't," Gabe assured her.

"Then never mind," Alma said cheerfully. "Call me if something comes up," she instructed just before she left the clinic.

"Yes, ma'am," he called after her.

"That's 'Deputy Ma'am' to you," she tossed over her shoulder with a laugh. And then the front door closed after her.

DAN FINISHED HIS examination as well as stitching up the gash on the blonde's forehead. His patient had remained unconscious through it all. For the time being, it was better that way for her. He was sufficiently certain that she would come around by-and-by.

Stripping off his rubber gloves and tossing them into the wastebasket, he came out into the waiting room to fill Gabe in on his findings.

"As far as I can tell, other than that gash on her forehead I had to stitch up, everything else seems all right. But I still think, just to be safe, she should get a CT scan of her head, make sure that there's no internal bleeding that we're overlooking."

"Wouldn't there be other signs if there was internal bleeding?" Gabe asked. It seemed to him that there should be, but then, that was only a guess on his part.

"Yes, but not always," Dan told him. "Like that old saying goes, better to be safe than sorry."

Gabe shrugged. "I'm not going to argue that, but if she doesn't know who she is and she has no ID, she sure as hell doesn't have any medical insurance—"

"Don't worry, I've got this covered," he assured the town's newest deputy.

Gabe only accepted so much on faith, the rest he questioned. "How?"

Dan smiled. The man wasn't very trusting. He could relate to that. He'd been the same way before he came to Forever, holding everything suspect until proven otherwise. It was an exhausting way to live.

"I pulled a few strings. Turns out the head of the radiology department graduated in my class the same year I did. We even threw back a few together at a handful of parties." He saw Gabe's frown and guessed what the man was probably thinking. "Don't worry, this job keeps you sober."

Gabe took the man's word for it. "Did she wake up at all?" he asked.

Dan shook his head. "She's still unconscious, I'm afraid."

Gabe would have thought that the doctor would have looked a bit more concerned about that. "Shouldn't we be worried by now?" Gabe asked.

"Not necessarily, she's had—"

Whatever reassuring sentiment he was going to express was drowned out by the scream that pierced the air. It came from inside the exam room that Dan had just left.

"Maybe we should start worrying now," Gabe commented as both he and Dan rushed back into the exam room.

They found the woman standing unsteadily before a mirror, her hands braced on either side of it to keep from falling to the floor. The expression reflected back appeared absolutely horrified.

Seeing the men coming in behind her, the woman turned to face them. The movement was just a tad too sudden and it threw her equilibrium—still wobbly—off. She looked as if she was about to fall, but Gabe reached her first, catching hold of her and helping her remain vertical.

Her eyes were wild as they went from the man holding on to her, to the slightly shorter man in the white lab coat. It was obvious that she was trying to place them—and couldn't.

"Why did you scream? What's wrong?" Gabe asked her sharply.

He'd come very close to drawing his service revolver. He had a feeling that would have frightened the blonde even more. She needed to trust him if they were ever going to get to the bottom of this.

In response to his question, the woman pointed at the image in the mirror as if she was pointing at someone she didn't know. There was uncertainty in her voice as she asked, "That's me, isn't it?"

"Yes," Dan answered, his tone calm, low.

She continued staring as disbelief sank in. "I look like hell."

"That's because you've been through hell," Gabe replied.

A shaky sigh escaped her lips. Then, unable to stand what she saw, the blonde turned away and looked at the two men who'd burst into the room, searching their faces. "What happened to me?"

"You were in a car accident," Gabe said gently, mimicking the voice his brother Eli used when he was training the quarter horses he sold. "When I found you, your car was on the verge of going over into a ravine. You're a very lucky woman," he concluded.

She didn't know about that. Tears stung her eyes, but her rising anger kept them back.

"If I'm so lucky, why can't I remember anything?" she demanded. "Why don't I even know my own name or who I am?"

"Hysterical amnesia," Dan told her. Her eyes shifted toward him, waiting—hoping—for answers. *Any* answers. The desperation inside her needed something to hold on to. "It happens after an accident sometimes. Victims block things out until they can handle processing them."

"Victims," she repeated.

Was that what she was? A victim? Did she feel like a victim? she wondered, trying to examine her feelings. Nothing came to her. She honestly didn't know. What did victims feel like?

"Am I all right?" she asked the man in the white lab jacket.

"So far," he replied cautiously. "But Gabe is going to take you to the hospital, to make sure."

"Gabe?" she repeated. The name meant nothing to her. Should it have? "Who's Gabe?"

"That would be me." Gabe raised his hand a little, drawing her attention to him as he gave her his most reassuring smile.

## Chapter Four

She shifted her eyes from one man to the other and then back again, hoping for something. A glimmer of a memory, an elusive flash of recognition, *anything*.

But there was nothing. Not so much as a hint of a hint.

"When is my memory going to come back?" she asked the doctor.

Right now, she felt like an empty vessel. She had no memories to access, no thoughts to fill her head. Nothing but a vast wasteland stretched before her, leading nowhere, involving nothing. The loneliness of that was almost unbearable.

"That's hard to say," he told her honestly. "It varies from person to person. You could remember everything in a few hours, or—"

"Or?" she prompted, battling back an ever-growing sense of desperation. Was it purely due to her wanting to remember?

Or did it involve something she wanted to forget? She just didn't know.

"Or you could never remember. But that's rather rare," he added.

"But it does happen," she pressed, not wanting him to sugarcoat anything.

She did her best to find a way to brace herself for never getting beyond this moment right now, and yet how could she since she had nothing to draw upon?

"Rarely," Gabe emphasized, speaking up. He noticed the look that Dan gave him. *Probably wondering where I got my medical degree,* Gabe thought. But he just couldn't let that devastated expression on her face continue. "No point in dwelling on possible worst-case scenarios. If it turns out to be that way, you've gained nothing by making yourself miserable," he explained. "And if it doesn't, well, then you've wasted a lot of precious time anticipating something that turned out not to happen."

A pragmatic thought rose to the fore—was she like that at heart? Or did this reaction just naturally evolve from her form of resignation? Again, nothing answered her silent query.

"From where I'm standing," she told Gabe, "looks to me like I've got nothing *but* time to waste."

"You're not going to be wasting time," Gabe told the blonde cheerfully. "You're coming with me, remember? To Pine Ridge Memorial to see what they have to say about all this."

It felt as if her head was spinning around in endless circles and she just wasn't making any headway. Both Gabe and the doctor seemed to be nice, but were they? And why were they so willing to go out of their way for her like this?

"Do I know either one of you?" she asked, looking from one face to another again.

But her reaction to either man was just the same as it had been a moment earlier. Neither one looked the least bit familiar, woke up nothing in her depleted memory banks.

"No, you don't," Dan answered for both of them.

Even in her present limited state, she knew that just didn't make any sense. "Then why are you doing this? Why are you taking me to a hospital in another town?"

"Because there is no hospital here," Dan replied matter-of-factly.

"Because you need help," Gabe told her almost at the same time.

It still didn't make sense to her. "And that's enough?" she questioned, puzzled.

Something told her that she wasn't accustomed to selfless people. That everyone was always out for their own special interests.

"It is for me," Gabe told her. "And for the doc," he added, nodding at the other man.

Damn but the way this woman looked at him made him want to leap tall buildings in a single bound and change the course of mighty rivers, just like the comic-book hero of long ago. The very thought worried him. And yet, he couldn't quite make himself back off. Couldn't just turn her over to either Alma or Joe.

This woman was his responsibility. *His* to help.

"Let's go," he urged the woman, putting his hand lightly to the small of her back. A thought occurred to him before they'd gone two steps. "Unless you'd like to get something to eat first?" he suddenly suggested. He looked over his shoulder at Dan to see if the doctor had any objections about the slight delay in getting to the hospital. "Would it make any difference if she got a bite to eat first before going to the hospital for those tests you ordered?"

During his exam, Dan had already checked her eyes extensively, using a probing light to determine the condition of her optic nerves. As a result, he was satisfied that there was no imminent danger, no swelling as far as he could see.

"I didn't detect anything that needed immediate attention," Dan told both of them.

Gabe had his answer and was pleased Dan sided with him. "All right, then, why don't we get you something to eat at Miss Joan's and then we'll be on our way." It wasn't a suggestion so much as a plan.

"Miss Joan's?" she repeated, confused. Everything sounded like a huge mystery, a question mark to her, and she'd already become weary of the blanks that she kept drawing.

The older woman had always been known to one and all as "Miss Joan." "Miss Joan owns the only diner in town. Best food you've ever had," he promised her.

"How would I know?" she answered, raising and lowering her shoulders in a vague, careless shrug. After all, she had nothing to compare it to. She might as well have lived in a cave these last—how old was she, anyway? Something else that she didn't know, she thought, frustrated.

"Trust me, it is," Gabe easily assured her as he ushered the woman out the door. Turning, he called out, "Thanks, Doc."

She took her cue from that, turning her head as well and calling out, "Yes, thank you."

With a quick wave, Dan turned back to go inside the clinic just as he saw two of his patients heading toward the building.

*Trust me.*

That was what the tall, dark-haired cowboy had just said. Why did that make her uneasy? Did she know him, after all? Was he not trustworthy?

Or was this uneasy feeling generated by someone else? Someone who she couldn't summon up in her defunct memory?

She stopped just as he brought her back to the passenger's side of his truck.

Gabe noted the tension in her shoulders. "Something wrong?"

"Other than everything being a perfect blank?" she asked him. It was hard to keep the bitterness out of her voice.

"Other than that," he allowed with a slight nod of his head.

Okay, he asked for it, she thought. "You said 'trust me.'"

He was still waiting. "Yes?" Did the phrase have any special significance to her?

"Can I?" she asked bluntly, adding, "Should I?"

"Yes and yes," Gabe answered easily. "Ask anyone, they'll tell you the same thing. You can trust me."

The testimony of strangers didn't mean anything

to her. "But I don't know anyone," she said quietly as she got in.

"True," he allowed, getting in on his side. "But you're going to find that, in this world, you've got to let yourself trust someone. Otherwise, life gets too hard. Too lonely."

It already was too lonely, she thought.

Suddenly a shiver danced over her, coming from regions unknown. As she tried not to let it shimmy down her spine, she heard herself asking, "But what if it's the wrong someone? What if I trust the wrong person?"

*What if I have already?*

Gabe paused, his hand on the ignition key, and looked at her, trying to discern what was behind her question.

"Did you?" he asked. "Did you trust the wrong person?" Were things beginning to fall together—albeit haphazardly—for her? Or was she just tossing out questions, trying to see if anything stuck?

She pressed her lips together as tears of frustration suddenly gathered in her eyes.

Was that only frustration, or was there more to it than that? She didn't know and she was already so sick of that phrase floating through her head.

*She didn't know.*

Would she *ever* know? Would she ever know anything about *anything?*

The uncertainty was driving her crazy.

"I don't know." She shrugged her shoulders helplessly again. "But something *feels* that way," she found herself admitting.

Gabe merely nodded. This time, he turned on the engine. It rumbled to life.

"It'll come to you," he promised. "All of it. When you least expect it."

She slanted a glance at him. Was he talking down to her? Or was there experience on which to base his answer?

"How do you know?" she finally challenged, not wanting to come across like a simpleton, secretly hoping to be convinced.

"I just do," Gabe said easily. He smiled at her. "It's called faith."

Did she have that? Did she have any faith? she wondered. She hoped so. She needed something to hang on to, she thought in desperation. So, for now, maybe it would be faith.

Faith in the man who was sitting beside her. A man who, though she really didn't remember it, apparently had saved her life.

"Okay," she said quietly. "I'll have faith."

Her answer surprised him, but he made a point of not showing her that.

"Good."

He'd wanted to insert her name here, except that there was no name to use. She hadn't had any sort of identification on her—no driver's license, no social security card, no well-creased love letter addressed to her hidden in the pocket of her black dress.

And if there had been any form of ID in the vehicle, most likely it was now burned to a crisp—as she almost was.

"I need something to call you," he told her. Even as he said it, he began going through possible names and rapidly discarding them for one reason or another. And then he had it. Just like that. "I know, how about Angel?"

"Angel?" she repeated, testing it out on her ear. Like everything else, it didn't seem familiar, but she liked the sound of it. "Why Angel?"

"Because you look like one," he answered simply. "At least, like one of the angels I used to picture when I was a kid," he told her with an affable grin.

"Angel," she said again, and then nodded. It had a nice ring to it. "All right. I guess you can call me that."

"Just until you remember your real name," he emphasized. Although he had a hunch it wasn't going to be as good as "Angel."

She looked at him, wishing she could believe what he'd just said. Why was it so easy for him and so hard for her?

"You really think I will?" she asked him.

There wasn't so much as a second's hesitation on his part. He saw no point in trying to hedge or qualify his words. This woman didn't need hesitation. She needed someone to believe *for* her until she could believe for herself.

"Yes, I really think you will. Hey," he spoke up with enthusiasm, "that's nice."

She looked around, but saw nothing unusual and had no idea what he was referring to. "What is?" she finally asked.

Easing to a stop at the light, he took the opportunity to look at her again. "You just smiled."

She wasn't aware of doing that. "I did?"

Even as she asked, she ran her fingertips along her lips to see if they were curving. And they were. She took solace in that and grew momentarily hopeful.

"You did," he confirmed. "You should do that more often," Gabe encouraged. "It lights up your whole face. Like an angel's," he added with a wink.

Something fluttered in her stomach when he did that. It mystified her even as she found herself enjoying it.

She had no idea what to make of any of it.

The diner was just beyond the next stop sign.

"Well, we're here," he told her, coming to a stop in one of the diner's designated parking spaces.

"Where's 'here'?" she asked, cocking her head as she peered through the windshield.

"Miss Joan's diner," he told her, unbuckling his seat belt and getting out.

Rather than head straight for the diner's door, Gabe rounded the hood of his vehicle and opened the door on Angel's side. He offered her his arm and stood waiting to help her out.

Though her memory continued to be a complete devastating blank, some distant instinct whispered that this wasn't what she was accustomed to. That having someone open the door for her and help her out of a vehicle was a completely new experience for her.

What a very strange thing to catch her attention, she thought, walking through the door of the diner as Gabe held it open for her.

Unlike the bone-chilling temperature outside, the inside of the diner embraced her with warmth the moment Gabe closed the door behind him.

Warmth and the scent of—

Fried chicken?

Angel stopped moving toward the counter for a moment, stunned by what was, she realized, her first fragment of a memory.

Gabe was immediately at her side, looking to see what had caught her attention. Nothing out of the ordinary popped up. But, he realized, that was *his* ordinary. It might not be hers.

"What's wrong?" Gabe asked. The expression on her face was difficult to place.

Angel turned toward him and said, "Fried chicken. I smell fried chicken."

There was mounting excitement in her voice, the way there might have been in the voice of the fifteenth century Spanish explorer Ponce de Leon the moment he realized that he'd stumbled across the long-missing Fountain of Youth in Florida.

"That's because that's the special of the day," Miss Joan informed her, calling out the information from her place behind the counter.

In the past few months, Miss Joan had finally broken down and married the man who'd been courting her for longer than anyone could remember. But, wedding or no wedding, everyone still called her Miss Joan. And Joan Randall Monroe definitely would not have had it any other way.

"C'mon over here, darlin'," she called, beckoning

Angel over to her. "Pull up a stool and rest yourself. I'll bring you a plate of chicken that'll make you swear you've died and gone to heaven." She paused a second before heading to the kitchen. "White or dark?" Miss Joan asked.

Angel looked at the still-attractive strawberry blonde blankly. "Excuse me?"

"What's your preference, darlin'?" Miss Joan rephrased her question. "Do you like white meat or dark meat better?"

Angel blew out an edgy breath. Even *that* was a mystery to her. What kind of a woman didn't know if she liked white meat or dark meat?

"I don't know," she answered unhappily.

As if not knowing was perfectly plausible, Miss Joan never missed a beat. "Then I'll bring you both." But before leaving, her almost-violet eyes shifted toward Gabe. "And you, handsome? What'll you have?"

"Dark," he said with finality. "And if you don't mind, make both to go."

Miss Joan looked from Gabe to the young woman beside him and then shook her head, as if mystified at the way any mind under fifty worked. "A little cold to be having a picnic, isn't it?"

"No, no picnic," he told her. "We're on our way to Pine Ridge."

Gabe thought nothing of sharing that sort of information with Miss Joan. Everyone did. Besides, the woman had a way of finding things out whether or not she was directly told. This just wound up saving time for both of them.

"Nothing wrong, I hope," Miss Joan said sympathetically. No one went to Pine Ridge unless it was to utilize the services of the hospital located in that town.

This time Gabe decided to just leave a vague response to her query but it was Angel who spoke up. "I don't know who I am."

To their surprise, Miss Joan took the response in stride. She merely nodded and chuckled. "A lot of that going around, darlin'," she assured Angel. "Don't let it worry you."

The woman probably meant something of the ordinary variety, Angel thought, like a person trying to "find" themselves. She wished that was her problem instead of the one she faced.

"No, I don't remember anything."

Miss Joan thought of the memories that crowded her brain, as well as a couple in particular that had, until her recent marriage, haunted her nights.

An enigmatic smile played on her thin lips. "Sometimes, honey, it's better that way."

That same strange chill slid down Angel's back, as if in response—and agreement—to what the outgoing woman had just said.

Now what did *that* mean? Angel couldn't help wondering.

## Chapter Five

"So, according to the CT scan, there's no damage?" Gabe asked Dr. Thom Holliman, the tall, imposing radiologist.

He and Angel had been at Pine Ridge Memorial Hospital for the better part of the day, during which time she'd been seen by a neurologist and had undergone several tests, the last of which had been a head CT scan.

As a favor to Dan, who had gone to medical school with the radiologist, Dr. Holliman had put a rush on the CT scan and had then personally interpreted the findings—or as it turned out, lack thereof.

Dr. Holliman shook his head, an action which caused his thick, dark brown hair to fall into his piercing dark blue eyes.

"No swelling, no indication of any bruising, or bleeding," the physician replied matter-of-factly. "Just that bump she sustained when she hit her head on the steering wheel, was it?"

The last was a question, since Holliman had just skimmed over the details of the car accident. Gabe had been the one to fill in the description because Angel still had no recollection of what had happened just prior to her temporarily regaining consciousness in Gabe's vehicle.

"Steering wheel," Gabe confirmed. The air bag hadn't deployed on impact, leaving Angel even more vulnerable. Luckily she hadn't sustained any more damages than she did. "So that's it?" he pressed the radiologist, repeating, "No damage?"

"You sound disappointed," Dr. Holliman observed. "Most people see this as good news."

Gabe didn't want the doctor to misunderstand. "It is, but—"

Gabe got no further in his explanation. Angel spoke up, interrupting him.

"If there's no sign of any injury to my brain, why can't I remember anything?" she asked. "Why can't I at least remember my own name?"

"You do remember some things," Dr. Holliman pointed out.

How could he say that? Her mind was as blank as a white sheet of paper.

"Like what?" Angel asked.

"Like all those things that you do automatically and take for granted." The skeptical look on her face had him elaborating. "How to walk, how to talk, how to dress yourself—those are all skills that, had you had a brain injury, you might not recall how to do. As for your recollection of who you are—"

She wanted the doctor to understand the full magnitude of the problem. It wasn't just her name. "And where I came from. Who my parents are and the thousand and one other details that go into forming memories as well as filling up my life. I don't remember *any* of that," she stressed.

Dr. Holliman inclined his head indulgently. "As to that, it could all very well be a matter of hysterical amnesia."

The assessment felt like a put-down to her. "I'm not hysterical," she told him, doing her best to sound calm, although it was getting more and more difficult for her. There was a wall of panic just beyond her calm facade. "I'm just empty. Completely empty."

The description was both a statement and a plea, the latter addressing the fact that she desperately needed something to help her find a way to regain what she had lost.

As Dr. Holliman stood regarding her thoughtfully, neither he nor Angel noticed that Gabe had taken a few steps back from them.

The next moment, Gabe called out, "Hey, Angel, catch." As he voiced the instruction, he tossed a small ball of aluminum foil toward her. The foil came from the take-out lunch he'd gotten at Miss Joan's diner and brought with him on the trip to the hospital. He hadn't realized until a couple of minutes ago that after balling it up he'd shoved it into his pocket.

Reacting, Angel's hand shot out to catch the small, shiny ball before it hit her or fell to the hospital floor. Still holding it in her hand, she looked at Gabe as if he'd lost his mind. Why was he throwing balled-up aluminum foil at her?

"What are you doing?" she asked, clearly surprised by his action. She threw the aluminum ball back to him.

He caught it easily. "Congratulations, you're right-handed," he told her, this time tossing the crushed aluminum ball into the wastebasket.

"What?" Angel looked at him, confused.

With a grin, he began to explain. Out of the corner of his eye, he saw the doctor nodding in approval. The man obviously understood what he'd tried to do.

"When I tossed that ball at you, you reached for it with your right hand. You did it automatically, without thinking. That means you're right-handed." Gabe could see what she was thinking, that there was a whole host of things she wanted to know about herself before finding out which hand she used to pick up her fork. Gabe lifted his shoulders in a good-natured shrug. "Gotta start somewhere, right?"

Gabe *was* right and she was acting like a petulant child, Angel thought. God, she hoped she wasn't one of those spoiled brats who expected to have everyone focusing their attention only on her, granting whatever wish she made.

The next moment, even that thought had her heartening just a little. The simple fact that she was aware of people like that meant that things *were* coming back to her, just not nearly as fast and furious as she would have liked. Still, baby steps were still steps.

"Right," she acknowledged. "Gotta start somewhere," she echoed.

"Well, I have more than half a dozen X-rays, MRIs and CT scans waiting for my attention," Holliman announced, signaling an end to the meeting. "I hope this reassures you two a little," he added, then reached into his left breast pocket and took out a card. "If you find you need something further, or if you experience any complications, feel free to give me a call."

"Complications?" she echoed, looking down at the business card he had just handed her. The word sounded ominous to her. "What sort of complications?" she asked.

"Complicated ones" was all Holliman had time to answer before hurrying back through the swinging doors that separated the people in the waiting room from the actual area where the tests were performed.

Gabe could see that she was disappointed. He supposed he couldn't blame her. She wanted a solution, a clear-cut reason *why* she had lost her memory. And then, she wanted to do whatever was necessary to fix that and get her memory back.

Except it wasn't that easy.

Which in turn had to be very frustrating to her.

"Focus on the positive side," he advised as he opened the door that led out into the long corridor and held it for her. "There's no brain damage, no abscess or lesion, nothing ruptured."

That all sounded well and good—except for the fact that she was still very much in the dark. "No rupture," she repeated. "The screen just went blank." There was a touch of sarcasm in her voice.

That was one way of putting it, he supposed. "Right. But since there's no problem with the wiring, the picture'll come back on. You just have to give it time."

She nodded, knowing he was right. Still, that didn't

make waiting any less difficult. "It would be a lot easier to do if I knew how much time I have to give it."

"That's simple," he said cheerfully. When she looked at him quizzically, he added, "You have to give it until the picture comes back."

"Very funny," she retorted in a tone that said the exact opposite.

"Just trying to lighten things up a little," he told her. *And so far, I'm not doing all that well,* he thought. "Did you know that doctors believe that laughter really *is* the best medicine?"

She laughed shortly as they walked through the maze of hospital corridors, heading toward the main entrance/exit. The parking lot where he'd left his truck was just beyond that.

"Bet the pharmaceutical companies don't want that getting around or else they'd be out of business. What?" Angel asked when she saw the satisfied expression on his face.

"See? Something else you know."

Had she missed something? What was he referring to? "What do I know?" she asked.

"You know about pharmaceutical companies enough to form an opinion."

And more than just in passing, would be his guess. Most people said "drug companies." Referring to them as "pharmaceutical companies" could mean that she had some sort of connection to that field. She could be a researcher or even a sales rep for one of companies, or know someone who was. It might give them a starting point to begin their search for her name.

Angel opened the truck's passenger door and got in. She slanted a glance in his direction as she pulled out the seat belt. "That's really reaching."

"Maybe not as much as you think," Gabe countered as he got in on his side.

She supposed he had a point. Leaning back in her seat, she secured the seat belt and then let out a long breath. Gabe started up the truck.

"Now what?" she asked.

That was simple enough. "Now we drive back to Forever."

For a second, she looked at him, confused by his answer. And then she remembered. "That's the town's name, right?"

"Right," Gabe answered with a grin.

"Forever," Angel repeated, rolling the name along her tongue. "Is there some kind of legend that goes along with that name?"

In no time at all, they'd reached Pine Ridge's town limits. Gabe thought for a moment. "I think the original founder fell in love with the countryside and said to his wife that he hoped that it would stay like this forever, that civilization with its progress and its grimy fingerprints would just bypass them."

That sounded incredibly hokey even to someone with no memory, Angel couldn't help thinking.

"Seriously?" she pressed. And then she saw that the corners of Gabe's mouth were curving ever so slightly. He was pulling her leg. "You just made that up, didn't you?" she accused.

"See?" he pointed out. "And now you remember how to read people."

She didn't see it that way. "Not people," Angel corrected. "You."

Despite her protest, Gabe saw no contradiction. "Well, the last I checked, I do fall into that category," he told her.

"But you're not typical," she protested with feeling that surprised her.

They were traveling at a steady speed now and the road was wide open before them. Gabe looked at her pointedly for a brief moment.

"And you would know that how?" he prodded.

"Because…"

Her voice trailed off, losing its steam. She realized that she had no explanation, no way to answer his question. All she had, she became aware, was just the faintest glimmer of a feeling that this deputy, who had come to her rescue, who was even now putting himself out to help her regain her memory, was not like other men.

At least, not like other men who she knew…

What men *did* she know? Angel couldn't help wondering as frustration continued to mount within her.

No names came to her, no faces. Nothing except some half-gelled, prickly feeling that refused to take on a recognizable form.

For all she knew, her reaction was based on just a guess on her part.

A frustrated sigh escaped her lips.

Without being fully aware of it, she fisted her hands in her lap. An overwhelming feeling of being trapped within this wall-less world with no other inhabitants save for her all but cut off her air and threatened to strangle her.

"Just because," Angel finally told him helplessly.

To her surprise, Gabe laughed softly.

Almost immediately she felt her back going up. Okay, something else to know about herself. She didn't like being laughed at.

"What's so funny?" she challenged.

"'Just because,'" he said her words back to her. "You answered with the exact same argument that my sister uses when she can't come up with something concrete to use."

He had a sister. Why did she feel she was supposed to know that? Had he already mentioned her? Or had she seen her?

Was it *ever* going to get any clearer, or at least less obscure? Or was she always going to have this haze inside her brain?

"Your sister?" she asked, hoping he'd offer a little enlightenment without her having to play more word games. His cheerful approach was beginning to grate on her nerves.

Or maybe her nerves were in a state because she found herself depending on this man and she didn't like that feeling.

Dependence led to entrapment, or disappointment. Or both.

How did she *know* that?

There were no answers, just more and more questions, it seemed.

Gabe nodded, his manner neither condescending nor impatient. "You met her earlier. She was the other deputy who came with Mick, the mechanic who towed away your car," he added when he saw that the man's name meant nothing to her.

"My car," she repeated, waiting for some sort of image to occur to her.

It felt as if she was straining her brain, but she continued to focus, trying to summon the image up, to have something come to her that at least felt as if it was vaguely familiar.

With a sigh, Angel surrendered with a shake of the head. Pointless. Gabe could have been talking about an old Roman chariot for all the difference it made.

Okay, she needed help here, Angel decided. She forced herself to ask, "What did it look like?"

"Like a piece of charcoal last I saw it."

Gabe knew that wasn't being very helpful, but he had to confess that before the explosion that had reduced Angel's vehicle to a charcoal briquette, he'd been so focused on getting her out of the precariously perched car that he hadn't noticed any actual details about the vehicle.

He thought back to the scene now, doing his best to remember when he'd first glimpsed the tottering sedan. "White—I think," he qualified. "Does that do anything for you?"

Angel shut her eyes, thinking that might help. It didn't.

Opening her eyes again, she looked at him and shook her head. The sigh came on its own accord. She was sighing more and more today, she thought. But who could blame her?

"Nothing," she told him.

"Why don't you try again later?" he advised. "A lot of times people remember things when they stop trying so hard to remember them. It'll come to you, probably in the middle of the night, or something equally as inconvenient."

Angel doubted that she was *ever* going to remember anything. It caused her to shrug helplessly in response to his advice.

"I guess I don't have a choice," she told him, resigning herself to this life in limbo that was staring her in the face.

"You always have a choice," Gabe contradicted. "Just sometimes it doesn't jump up, waving flags and grabbing your attention, that's all."

She settled back in her seat. Dusk was beginning to creep up, coloring the scenery in darkening hues. "So it's back to…Forever?" she asked, remembering what he'd just said in response to her question about their next step.

"Unless you have another suggestion," he told her, letting her know that he was perfectly open to anything she might have in mind.

Angel shook her head in response. That was the problem. Try as she might, no other destination came to her. No town, no shop, no person. It was as if her mind had been sent into solitary confinement.

And her fate was entirely in this man's hands. A man she hadn't even *known* early this morning.

"And what happens when I get to Forever?" she asked him.

He pretended to think it over before saying in a perfectly serious voice, "Well, we sell you into bondage and you have to work for Mick for the rest of your life." That was as long as he could maintain a straight face. Then he asked her, "What do you mean, what happens when you reach Forever?"

"I mean, well, where am I going to stay?' she asked, tripping over her own tongue. "I don't have any money to pay for the motel room."

She didn't understand why he laughed at that until he told her, "That's not exactly a problem since we don't have a motel in Forever."

Every place had motels—didn't they? Just where *was* she and why had she come here? It didn't seem like a place she'd choose.

*Oh, right,* she mocked herself. *And your tastes run to what? Palaces?*

"What do you have?" she asked gamely.

"Tourists who pass through on their way to somewhere else." Which was true. Outside of Miss Joan's cooking, the town boasted of nothing special.

So, they did have people passing through the town. "Where do visitors stay?" she asked gamely.

"Usually with whoever they're visiting," Gabe told her.

She looked at him sharply, but he wasn't saying that to tease her. "You're kidding."

"On occasion," he allowed, then qualified, "but not this time. Why?"

Didn't he see the problem? "Well, where am I going to stay?"

"I've got a pup tent we can set up in the backyard," he quipped. And then he smiled at her. "Don't worry, we'll work something out."

Suspicion rose in her eyes before she was even aware of it forming. "And by 'we' you mean…?" She left the end of the sentence open for him to fill in.

"You, the sheriff, my sister. Maybe Miss Joan." Although since the woman had gotten married, she wasn't nearly as available to put people up the way she had previously been. The doctor's wife, Tina, had stayed with Miss Joan for quite a while before Dan had come into town and promptly fallen for her. "Me," he added in case she thought he was distancing himself from her.

Her eyes darted toward him. "Oh," Angel murmured.

He didn't know if the information comforted her or agitated her. He couldn't tell by the single-word response. For now, though, maybe it was for the best to leave the matter alone. Angel had enough to deal with without his quizzing her.

Turning on the radio to combat the silence before it became overpowering, Gabe kept on driving.

## Chapter Six

Angel was positive that she was far too wired to fall asleep tonight—possibly ever. Wound up as tightly as a coil in an old-fashioned box spring mattress, if anyone had asked her, Angel would have sworn that sleep would elude her for a good long while to come.

This despite the fact that, along with being wired, she felt incredibly drained.

She had initially closed her eyes to rest them because it felt as if they were wearing themselves out, staring at a world and at people that were equally unfamiliar to her. Toward the end, her lids actually felt as if they were burning.

Now, of course, there was just miles and miles of miles and miles. Nothing differentiated one section of land from another as they drove back to Forever from Pine Ridge.

*Back* to Forever. As if that was where she'd come from, Angel mocked herself. She didn't belong in Forever. And she was getting to believe that she didn't belong anywhere.

The restlessness that insisted on haunting her was

back in spades. A restlessness that came from not knowing.

Would she *ever* know where she belonged? Or, for that matter, even what kind of a person she was? It was awful, not knowing.

Was she kind, heartless, intelligent, lazy, a little of all of that—or what?

As before, no answers came to her, not even so much as a vague hunch that she might be on the right path to discovery.

God, but she was getting tired of feeling like a living question mark.

So very tired...

ANGEL HAD BEEN QUIET for the past ten, twelve miles Gabe thought, glancing toward the woman to his right. Were things coming back to her? Or was it frustration that kept her silent?

Whether he liked it or not, because he'd rescued her, he felt responsible for this lost woman.

Gabe wasn't the type who immediately shouldered responsibility with gusto and enthusiasm, but neither did he attempt to shrug it off or hide behind some rock in an out-and-out attempt to avoid it. It was what it was and he accepted it. In some cultures, he knew, because he'd saved her, the woman he'd christened "Angel," her soul was his.

Just what he needed, he thought with a touch of cynicism, a spare soul to trip him up. These days, he wasn't all that certain what to do with his own, not after the way Erica had left him at such loose ends.

He'd never seen himself as some fancy-free play-boy, but neither had he thought of himself as being the marrying kind—at least, not until Erica had crossed his path. Suddenly the thought of settling down with a wife and two, three kids didn't seem so bad. As a matter of fact, it sounded pretty good.

Except now he wouldn't get to find out because Erica had decided she could "do better." Dumping him without warning, she'd turned around and made Seth Madden the center of her world.

Just like that.

Granted, Seth was a banker and came across more polished than he did, but hell, Seth had eyes that belonged to a flounder that had been dead for two days. Was that what Erica really wanted, a man with lifeless eyes?

Gabe couldn't manage to convince himself of that—and he definitely couldn't bring himself to either forgive Erica, or let the whole thing go.

He felt as if he was permanently stuck in limbo.

Probably not unlike Angel and her memory loss.

He tried to picture himself in that sort of a situation and found himself being very grateful that he *wasn't* in that sort of a situation.

"We're here," he announced.

By "here," Gabe meant that they had just crossed the town limits and were now officially in Forever.

"Angel? We're here," he repeated when he received no response in return. When she failed to say anything the second time, Gabe slowed the car down to almost a crawl—which was less than twenty miles an hour to his way of thinking—and looked at Angel's face more closely.

He forced himself not to get distracted by how very pretty she was and only think of her as someone who had had one *hell* of a day.

"Really awful to be you right now, isn't it?" he murmured softly in sympathy.

She seemed to be sound asleep, her head leaning slightly forward. Watching her, Gabe was fairly certain she was going to have a really bad crick in her neck to add to the litany of aches and pains that she would have tomorrow. All of which would be due to the car accident she'd barely survived.

"Angel?" he said softly, trying to rouse her but not startle her.

The only thing he received in reply was the sound of her even breathing.

Gabe frowned, thinking. He couldn't very well just leave her here, sleeping in his truck, but he felt bad about waking her up. If he did, she might wind up being awake all night.

Still, it was getting really cold and he couldn't just run the engine so that he could keep the heat on for her. Other than that being an impossibly expensive way to keep someone warm, there was also the very real danger of filling the inside of his vehicle with carbon monoxide.

Maybe she'd wake up on her own if he just gave her a little more time. It was worth a try.

With a shrug, Gabe drove the truck to his house.

His house.

That was still taking some getting used to. Originally

it was known as the old Douglas place. He'd bought it several months ago from Alec Douglas. The latter had returned to Forever to settle up his late father's affairs, sell the house and go back to his life in Virginia where he'd been working for the past ten years.

Both he and Alec had been happy with the deal that had been struck for the two-story house. True, the fifty-year-old house needed a lot of work, but like everyone who lived around here, he was handy, plus he didn't mind working with his hands. He found it therapeutic and it gave him something to do on his days off—when he wasn't helping out on the family ranch.

As long as he kept too busy to think, that was just fine with him.

Pulling up in front of the house now, Gabe left his truck parked to the left of the porch steps. He glanced at Angel again. The woman just kept right on sleeping.

Gabe got out of the vehicle, rounded the back and came up to the passenger door. Opening it, he paused for a second, debating his next move. With a shrug, he thought he'd try to wake her by gently shaking her shoulder.

When he did, she just kept right on sleeping as if he hadn't touched her at all.

"Damn, but you could probably sleep through a twister, couldn't you?" he marveled, murmuring the assessment under his breath.

Leaving her where she was for the moment, Gabe went up the steps to his front door, unlocked it and left it wide open. Angel was still asleep when he returned to the vehicle.

Her body probably needed to recharge itself, he reasoned.

Leaning over her, Gabe very carefully released the seat belt clip and unbuckled her. Then, as gently as possible, he picked her up from her seat and began to walk up the steps to his front door.

To his amazement, as he reached the top step, Angel continued sleeping. Not only that, but as he made his way into the house, the sleeping woman curled into him. A sigh that sounded suspiciously like contentment escaped her lips as she apparently made herself comfortable against his chest.

He caught himself looking down at her face. It was relaxed and there was almost a purity about it. He reasoned that, asleep, Angel didn't resort to a barrage of defense mechanisms.

This was the real woman, the one beneath the bravado. Soft, innocent. Relaxed.

He found himself intrigued.

Because he had just recently moved into the house, Gabe wasn't anywhere near finished furnishing the different rooms. To be honest, he had hardly gotten started.

So far, there was only one bed—his—and that was in the master bedroom. The other two bedrooms had a variety of things piled up in them, none of them meant to provide any kind of rest for the weary. In actuality, the exact opposite was true. Both rooms were in a state of varying degrees of chaos.

Since it had a bed, Gabe decided to give Angel his bedroom while he made himself as comfortable as possible on the secondhand sofa he'd picked up for his living room.

Gabe made his way up the stairs slowly, watching Angel's face as he went. Though her lashes seemed to flutter a little, she continued sleeping. When he finally set her down on top of the covers on his bed, it had no effect on her.

Angel went on sleeping.

A quirky smile curved his lips as he stepped back for a second. Taking the extra blanket he had folded at the foot of his bed, he spread it out and covered her.

She really did look like an angel, sleeping that way, he thought.

He hoped that the morning would turn out to be better for her. Maybe she'd even remember who she was.

People shouldn't be shut out of their own lives, he reasoned.

It occurred to him, as he all but tiptoed out of the room, that he was pretty damn tired himself. He hadn't exactly been sitting around these past eighteen hours, twiddling his thumbs.

Closing the door softly behind him, Gabe went downstairs.

As he passed by the kitchen, he glanced toward it out of habit. For exactly ten seconds, he considered making himself something to eat. But his need to sleep far outweighed his desire to eat. He made his way into the living room. Gathering the newspaper that was haphazardly strewn over the sofa, he dumped the pages onto the floor and sat down. The worn leather sofa creaked a little as it accepted his weight. Like the house, it was old, but comfortable.

Putting his muscle into it, he pulled off first one boot, then the other. He placed them on top of the newspapers so he could find them readily enough in the morning and lay down. No sooner had his head touched the flattened-out pillow in the corner than his cell phone began to both ring and buzz in his pocket.

He didn't know which he hated more, the ringing or the buzzing.

The cell phone was something he would have just as easily done without. But the phone had come with his badge and the job. It was the sheriff's belief that since the terrain they oversaw was so scattered and large, a cell phone—when the signal found it—was a good way to stay in touch. With that explained to him, Gabe couldn't just ignore the phone even though he had little use for it, or any of the other new "toys" out there. Electronic novelties carried absolutely no fascination for him.

Pulling the phone from his pocket, he pressed the accept button. "This is Gabe."

"Where *are* you?"

It wasn't Rick, it was Alma. And she sounded pretty miffed.

"Home," he told his sister. "Technically," he added before she could bombard him with any more questions, "my shift is over. I'm off the clock."

"That shouldn't stop you from swinging by the sheriff's office at the end of the day."

"It can," he contradicted, "since I got shanghaied

into being someone's fairy godmother," he informed his sister.

She supposed she was worrying too much about Gabe making a good impression. If Larry, the deputy whose place he was taking, decided for one reason or another not to return to Forever, she wanted Gabe to be the one to fill the position permanently. That started by making a good impression—every single day.

"How is she?" she asked about the woman who'd been placed in his care.

"Right now? Asleep," he told her. *Just like I'd like to be.*

There was a pause on the other end of the line and he knew that questions were popping up in his sister's mind like toast out of a squadron of toasters set on low.

"*Where* is she asleep?" he heard Alma finally ask.

"In a bed. I didn't think the rock garden was a good place to put her," he deadpanned.

Alma ignored his sarcasm, sailing right by it as if he hadn't even tapped into the tone. "*Your* bed?" she asked.

"Well, yeah, it's the only one I got in the house, remember?"

She knew the kind of man her brother was, so she didn't ask the one question that begged asking: *Where are* you *going to sleep?* Instead, she went to another line of questioning altogether. "Then I take it they didn't want to keep her overnight at the hospital?"

"No reason to." *Thank God,* he added silently. It would have been a hassle for him if they had. He would have either had to get a room at a local hotel, or driven back and forth from Pine Ridge twice. Neither of which appealed to him. "All the tests they took of her came back negative."

"But she still doesn't remember."

He could hear the frown in Alma's voice. "But she still doesn't remember," he echoed, confirming his sister's assumption.

"You didn't have to bring her to your place, you know. You could have brought her here," Alma told him.

He was in no mood to justify his actions to his sister right now. Lack of sleep made him less tolerant and more irritable.

"Made a spur-of-the-moment decision," he told her. "Angel fell asleep while we were driving back from Pine Ridge. I didn't have the heart to wake her up."

"Angel, huh? Well, I guess if you had to come up with a name, that's as good as any. But did it ever occur to you that she might have wanted you to wake her up?" Alma pointed out.

"Well, we won't know until she does, will we?" he countered. Tired of sparring, however innocuously, with Alma, he asked, "Is there anything else? Because if there isn't, I'm pretty beat and I'd like to turn in. *On the sofa,*" he underscored in case she felt duty-bound to ask him where he was spending the night.

"Never doubted it for a moment," she said. "Go, get your beauty sleep, Gabe. By my count you're about three years behind and are getting to look pretty mangy and scary."

"I can always count on you to feed my ego," Gabe quipped. "Good night, Alma."

Not waiting for her response, he hung up. He didn't

want to give her any time to regroup and ask him about something else.

With a sigh that came from deep down in his bones, Gabe stretched out on the sofa. He pulled down the crocheted throw lying along the back of the sofa and wrapped it around himself to ward off the pending cold.

Gabe had always had the ability to fall asleep within three minutes of his head hitting anything that could remotely pass for a pillow. Tonight was no exception.

If anything, he was asleep in two minutes rather than three.

And he would have slept right through until morning—if the scream hadn't woken him up.

Scissoring apart a dream that evaporated the instant he opened his eyes, Gabe bolted upright, trying to separate reality from any remaining strands of his dream that might have somehow managed to linger around.

Confusion temporarily dimmed his ability to think.

That vanished the moment he heard the scream again. It wasn't bloodcurdling so much as profoundly heartbreaking.

And it was also not a dream. Both screams had come from upstairs.

Angel!

Gabe's feet hit the floor, running. He made it across the living room in record time, heading for the stairs. Taking them two at a time, he quickly made it up the stairs and to his room.

It didn't even occur to him to stand on ceremony and knock, or call through the door. Rules and polite behavior quickly died in the face of Angel's screams.

He threw open the door. A solid block of darkness met him. He felt the left wall for a light switch. Finding it, he flipped it to the up position.

It didn't really help all that much.

He blinked, trying to adjust his vision as he looked around. Angel wasn't where he'd left her. The bed was empty.

"Angel?" he called out. "Where are you? Why are you screaming?"

She didn't answer.

He found her huddled in the corner on the floor just beneath the window. There was a crescent moon out and an eerie yellow glow touched the windowsill. It seemed to heighten the aura of fear emanating from her.

"Angel?" he said, worried as he crossed to her. "Are you all right?"

Rather than answer, Angel looked up at him with enormous, frightened eyes. Gabe crouched down to her level. What had spooked her this way? If someone had tried to break in, he would have heard them.

He needed to calm her down, he thought. Otherwise, the situation could grow out of control.

"You're shaking like a leaf in the wind," he noted. "Why? What happened?"

As he tried to put his arm around her, Angel stiffened and pulled back.

Was she still asleep? He'd heard that people could look awake when they really weren't. Sleepwalking didn't just involve walking. It took in all facets of this strange condition.

Was she in the throes of some kind of a nightmare that was holding her prisoner?

"Angel, it's me," he told her as softly as possible. He refused to remove his hands from her shoulders. He saw it as the only way he could anchor her. "It's Gabe. You're in my house. You're safe," he said, then repeated with emphasis, "Safe. Do you understand?"

Angel struggled, trying to pull away again. And then she began to sob. Within a moment, she suddenly slumped against him, her sobs growing louder. And then they began to subside.

"Gabe?"

Did she recognize him, or had her nightmare somehow caused her to forget him, as well?

"Yes, Gabe. You know, the guy who's been hanging out with you all day, taking you to hospitals and fun places like that." And then he dropped the teasing tone. Instead, he lightly stroked her hair, still trying to calm her. "You had a nightmare."

"No, I—" She stopped abruptly. "A nightmare?" she repeated. She looked at him in wonder. "But it was so real."

Maybe this was the key they needed to unlock her memory. He loathed having her relive something that obviously terrified her, but if it meant that she could start to remember, Gabe felt that he had to try. "What was it about?"

Distress filled her eyes as she looked up at him and realized, "I can't remember."

# Chapter Seven

The next moment, in a fit of pure frustration as angry tears filled her eyes, Angel fisted her hand and hit it against the wall.

"I can't remember, I can't remember, I can't remember," she cried, her voice growing more agitated with each repetition.

Moved and almost overwhelmed with sympathy, Gabe enfolded her in his arms. Angel was too weary and too drained to struggle and pull away.

"Then don't try," Gabe told her gently.

Desperately searching for a clearing in the fog that had laid siege to her mind, Angel raised her head to look up at him, confused. Was he really telling her to give up?

"What?"

"Then don't try," Gabe repeated. "Just for now," he advised, "just let yourself be."

"But who *is* 'myself'?" she cried. Didn't he see? That was the problem. She didn't know. How could she be herself when she didn't know what that meant, what it involved.

To her surprise, he didn't shrug or dismiss her exasperated question. Instead, looking directly into her eyes, he gave her an answer.

"A beautiful woman who survived a horrific accident that could have very easily been fatal. You're a survivor," he told her. "For now, that'll be enough. We'll build on that."

"'We'?" she questioned. How could there be a "we" when she was so very alone?

Gabe nodded. "You and me. And everyone else in town." He smiled as he saw the skepticism entering her eyes. "Forever's that kind of a town. People like helping their neighbors whenever they can."

He made it sound like a perfect place. She would have loved to believe him. But there was just one thing wrong with his assumption.

"I'm not a neighbor," she pointed out.

His eyes continued to hold hers. "You're here, aren't you?"

Of course she was here, she thought. He knew that. "Yes, but—"

Gabe cut in, stopping her right there. "People in Forever don't need anything more than that. So—" a whimsical smile curved Gabe's lips as he looked at her "—are you planning on staying down here until morning, or would you like to get up? Maybe lie down and get a little more sleep?" he suggested, nodding at the bed.

She looked back at the bed she'd run from in her terrified, semiwakeful state and let out a ragged breath. "I don't think I can sleep," she told him.

"Okay." Rising to his feet, Gabe extended his hand

to her. After a beat, she took it and allowed him to pull her to her feet. "I can make us some coffee," he offered.

For the first time, questions that had nothing to do with the past she couldn't remember occurred to Angel. She looked around at her surroundings. "Is this your place?"

He nodded, then apologized. "Sorry about the mess. I just moved here."

He'd tendered the explanation that, according to Alma, was getting a little frayed around the edges since he'd made absolutely no headway in organizing his things since the first day he brought them into the house. Cleaning had never been one of his attributes and most likely never would be, but for now, Angel didn't need to know that about him.

"Why here?" Angel asked.

"Because the owner gave me a good deal on the place and I—"

Angel shook her head. He'd misunderstood her question. Small wonder, she thought, since she'd only given him a snippet of what had occurred to her in her mind.

"No, why did you bring me here?"

"You fell asleep in the car on the way back. You looked so peaceful, I didn't want to disturb you. I figured it was just easier to carry you into my house than go knocking on Alma's or Miss Joan's door to stay there."

She turned to look at him. His description of the events took her by surprise. "You *carried* me into the house?"

He laughed. Why would that surprise her? Other

than waking her up—which he was trying *not* to do—
that had been his only option.

"Well, my magic wand's in the shop and dragging
you from the car into the house by your hair just didn't
seem like the way to go, so yeah, I carried you," he told
her. "Why?"

"No reason." She didn't want to tell him that the
thought of his carrying her like some princess in a fairy
tale seemed so incredibly sweet, not to mention roman-
tic.

It wasn't until almost a minute later that she realized
his words struck a faraway chord in the barren wasteland that comprised her mind. She tried to make it come
closer, but couldn't.

Had someone carried her up the stairs before? Or
was she just imagining it?

"It just sounded…" Her voice trailed off for a moment before she concluded, "Familiar."

Gabe fought the urge to press, to ask her what else
might have sounded familiar. That would have definitely been the wrong way to proceed. What she needed
right now was to give herself time to heal, to relax, and
maybe then she would remember something more.

Until then, they both had to remain patient—most
of all, *he* had to remain patient because as far as he
was concerned, it was up to him to set the pace for her.

So, reining in his curiosity, Gabe nodded and said,
"Good. Something to build on *later*." He emphasized
the last word. "Now, would you like that cup of coffee?"

Angel looked at the bed again. "No, maybe you're

right," she allowed. "Maybe I should try to get some more sleep."

"Okay. Sounds good," he agreed readily. Beginning to make his way toward the door, he said, "I'll be just downstairs if you need me." He pointed in the general direction of the door even as he started to walk out.

"Gabe?"

Something in her voice stopped him and he turned from the door. "Yes?"

"Would you…" She licked her lips, lips that suddenly seemed so very dry to her. "Would you…" She began again, only to have the words freeze in her throat. She felt awkward and uncomfortable about the request she wanted to make. A request to a man who'd virtually been a stranger to her less than a day ago.

She had no right to ask this of him, Angel told herself.

It didn't take a genius to figure out what she was trying to say, Gabe thought. He could remember a time, when he was a very young boy, when he had been afraid of the dark. In a way, this was a little like that.

"Would you like me to stay until you fall asleep?" he asked kindly.

Relief instantly washed over her features. "Would you?"

He felt something stir inside of him. That protective streak he was trying to ignore. She just seemed to keep bringing it out.

"Sure." As she lay down on the bed, Gabe sank down on the floor, his back against the bed. There was no chair in the room. "I wasn't planning on going anywhere, anyway," he told her.

She was more tired than she realized. And having him here allowed her to relax enough to sleep.

"Gabe?"

He could hear the drowsiness creeping into Angel's voice. "Yes?"

"I'm glad you were the one who saved me."

Her remark made him smile. "Yeah." He laughed softly. "Considering that the alternative's pretty gruesome."

He didn't understand again, Angel realized hazily. "No, I'm glad *you* were the one who saved me," she repeated with fading emphasis.

Within a few moments, secure in Gabe's presence that he would be there to ward off her demons, Angel fell asleep.

An enigmatic smile played on his lips as Gabe twisted around and looked at her for a long moment.

"Yeah," he finally replied very quietly. "Me, too."

For a second, he thought about getting up and going downstairs, now that she was asleep. But if she woke up again and found herself alone, she might feel anxious or even threatened. He didn't want to chance that.

So, making himself as comfortable as he could, given the circumstances, Gabe rested his head against his raised knees, closed his eyes and waited for morning to come.

SOMETHING—A SCENT? aroma?—teased his senses, weaving its way into his consciousness.

With a start, Gabe woke up. It took him a second to orient himself. He was still on his bedroom floor, half leaning against the side of his bed. His limbs protested somewhat as he got to his feet. Falling asleep like that was definitely *not* the last word in comfort.

But that wasn't what was bothering him.

His bed was empty.

So was the room, he discovered as he quickly looked around it.

"Angel?" he called out.

His voice echoed back to him. There was no other response.

Had she taken off for some reason? Had something more actually frightened her last night, something that she *hadn't* for some reason elaborated on?

He needed to find her.

Already dressed, Gabe looked around for his boots amid the chaos on the bedroom floor until he remembered. His boots were still downstairs in the living room where he'd left them last night.

Hurrying down the stairs, Gabe became aware of the strong smell of coffee. Not just coffee but…bacon?

*That* was what had woken him up. The aroma of breakfast being made.

By the time he reached the bottom of the stairs, the sense of urgency that had initially propelled him had abated. Instead, he followed the invisible, aromatic trail to the kitchen.

And found Angel. She was up—and apparently cooking breakfast.

As subtly as he could, Gabe blew out a long breath of

relief, then crossed over to her at the stove. Unlike the bedlam that ensued whenever he cooked for himself, she seemed to be right at home in the kitchen.

"You're cooking," he marveled.

Startled by his presence, Angel swung around. Seeing Gabe, she flashed him an uneasy smile. "I hope you don't mind. This seems to relax me," she confessed. Like a puppy to a bowl full of treats, she'd found herself drawn to the kitchen pantry as well as the refrigerator. The rest had just happened. It was a little like being on automatic pilot.

"Mind?" he repeated, mystified. "Why should I mind? A. I like to eat and B. more important than that—" he grinned as he pointed out the obvious "—you remembered how to cook."

The second part of his assertion seemed to surprise her, as if she'd just realized that what he'd said was true.

A rather embarrassed, although pleased, smile curved the corners of her mouth. "I guess I did, didn't I?"

He looked over her shoulder. There were two skillets on the burners. The smaller one had the bacon in it. The larger skillet was exclusively devoted to an omelet she was in the middle of creating.

"You sure did," Gabe told her. "Not everyone takes on making an omelet the morning after they've lost their memory. Looks like the pieces are starting to come together for you."

"Yeah, but all the pieces have something to do with food," she lamented.

"Remember, you've gotta start somewhere," he reminded her of their earlier exchange. He paused by the coffeemaker and inhaled deeply. "The coffee smells great," he enthused.

Coffee—good coffee—was his personal weakness. Pouring himself a mug, he noted out of the corner of his eye that she was watching him. Apparently she was holding her breath until he took a sip. Which he did gamely. Unable to wait patiently any longer, Angel asked hopefully, "Good?"

"No," Gabe answered. Then, just as her face began to fall, he raised the mug in his hand high, as if to toast her with it. "It's *great*," he emphasized.

For the first time, he saw a glimmer of happiness enter her eyes. "Really?"

Gabe inclined his head. "Really," he assured her with feeling.

Leaning a hip against the counter, he took another sip of coffee—a long one this time—and watched with interest the way she wielded the large knife in her hand. She moved it rhythmically on the chopping block, turning a red pepper into confetti, cutting the sections into equal tiny pieces.

Observing the way her hands were moving came very close to watching poetry in motion.

"Maybe you're a professional," he guessed out loud.

Angel raised her eyes to his face, her hands stilled for a second.

"A what?" she asked warily.

"A professional. You know," he elaborated, "like a chef or one of those people they have on TV, hawking their cookbooks and trying to hook people on preparing meals their way."

Angel appeared skeptical, he observed, even though she never stopped chopping. She slid the resulting heap of finely sliced vegetables into the skillet. "You really think so?"

He answered her question with a question. "How does that knife feel in your hands?"

She'd instinctively selected it from his chopping block after quickly examining all the knives mounted in the block. This one looked up to the job. How she knew that, she hadn't a clue. But she'd been right.

Looking down at it now, she said, "Good," then added, "Like it belongs there."

Gabe nodded at the answer he'd expected. "Which makes you either a professional chef—or an apprentice ax murderer—and something tells me that it's probably not the latter."

When she laughed in response, pleasure wove through him. He liked the sound of her laughter.

It took Angel a few more minutes to finish making the omelet. Gabe was on his second mug of coffee and had done justice to three pieces of bacon, nibbling them to oblivion, when she transferred her creation onto a plate and then pushed it in front of him.

"Tell me what you think."

He heard the hopeful note in her voice. There was no way he was about to burst her bubble even if what she'd just made tasted like shoe leather left out in the sun for three days and stuffed with rotting rattlesnakes.

She was obviously making progress and he wanted to keep it that way.

"Well?" she asked as the first forkful slid between his lips.

To his relief, it definitely did *not* taste like three-day-old shoe leather stuffed with rotting rattlesnakes. Instead, magnificent tastes exploded on his tongue, tantalizing him.

He nodded with feeling. "You're definitely a professional." Setting aside the coffee mug, he drew the plate closer and began to eat in earnest. "This is really great. You've got a gift," he told her.

Angel hugged his words to her. They filled her insides like the first rays of sunshine rising after a long and dreary winter. Why hearing them from Gabe meant so much she wasn't able to explain, but there was no denying the end result.

"You really think so?" she pressed, barely able to suppress her enthusiastic reaction.

Rather than answer verbally, Gabe just nodded. He was too busy polishing off the rest of the omelet. As he ate, an idea came to him. And in its wake, a sense of relief along with it.

"Now I know what to do with you while I'm at work," he told her.

He'd been a bit concerned about that. Since he'd just begun to fill in for Larry, he couldn't exactly take off to watch over Angel, and yet he didn't feel that he should leave her by herself. She seemed a bit fragile to him and he was afraid that she might wind up losing the ground she'd gained so far.

Angel frowned slightly. She wasn't quite following him. "You want me to cook for you?"

Gabe held up his hand to keep her from making any more guesses until he could tell her himself. He didn't like to talk with his mouth full, but there was no way he was about to leave even so much as a single morsel on his plate.

"Not for me," he corrected, even though he had to admit that he was strongly tempted to keep her and her culinary talents all to himself. He couldn't remember when he'd eaten anything this good. "Miss Joan could use you in her kitchen. Eduardo, her short-order cook for what seems like the past century, told her he was retiring at the end of the month, which means that she has to find someone to take his place before then." He grinned at her as he reached for the last of his coffee. "I think you're about to solve her problem. It'll only be temporary," he added quickly, in case what he was saying made her feel hemmed in. "Just until you get your memory back and she finds someone. And who knows?" he posed. "Cooking for her might even help you get your memory back."

She looked at him hopefully. "Do you really think so?"

"Why not?" he asked. "Things never go according to plan. Sometimes they go better, sometimes worse, but always, it seems, at their own pace, not ours." Finished, he set down his mug, his eyes still on her. "How does that sound to you?"

Angel smiled warmly at him. "It sounds great," she told him. "Really great."

He found himself fascinated with the look that came into her eyes.

## Chapter Eight

"So it's all right with you?"

Gabe looked at Miss Joan closely as he asked the question an hour later.

He and Angel were in the diner, standing off to the side of the counter and trying to keep out of the way of a steady stream of breakfast "regulars." The latter group were coming in to jump-start their day with Miss Joan's famous coffee and one of Eduardo's special breakfast platters.

"Yes." Miss Joan gave him a look that said he should know better than to think that she wouldn't agree to this. "Even if you weren't my brand-new granddaughter's brother," she added with a smile.

Having married Harry Monroe, she now had the family she'd been denied for so long. And with Harry's grandson marrying Alma, that made Alma's five brothers part of her family, as well. It filled a need within her that had gone begging far too long.

Miss Joan glanced around Gabe's shoulder at the young woman he'd first brought in with him yesterday. "With Eduardo running out on me, I've got to find someone to take his place."

"I am *not* running out on you, old woman," the cook spoke up from the kitchen where he was furiously working to keep up with the incoming flood of orders. "I am *retiring,*" he declared, stressing every single letter of the word. "Before I fall on the floor, dead, because you have worked me to that state. A man has a right to live and enjoy himself in his last few years."

Speculation went that Eduardo was actually younger than Miss Joan, but no one really knew for sure and, in the interest of peace, no one was about to bring that matter up with Miss Joan.

"Huh." Miss Joan blew out a breath, exasperated. "You're going to live to be over a hundred, Eduardo, and we all know it, so stop trying to paint yourself as some kind of a victim. You go through with this, and you'll go stir-crazy before your first month of 'retirement' is up," she predicted. Miss Joan leveled her gaze at Angel, then nodded toward the swinging doors that led to the kitchen. "Go in and get yourself an apron and show me what you've got, girl. And don't let that old man scare you," she added, raising her voice so that Eduardo heard. "He's all bark and no bite."

"Ha! You should talk," Eduardo retorted. "You yap enough to give a man a headache forever!"

Gabe looked from the narrow space above the counter, where all the orders were placed once they were filled, to Miss Joan. He lowered his voice and said, "You're really going to miss that old man, aren't you?"

Miss Joan shook her head, not in denial but in sad anticipation of what was to come in a far too close future if Eduardo actually *did* retire.

"More than words can say," she whispered back. "But don't let him know," she warned, slanting a look over her shoulder toward the kitchen.

Gabe grinned. "I've got a feeling that he already knows, Miss Joan."

But Miss Joan wasn't all that convinced. "If he thought that, he'd say it, believe me. Hell, he'd crow it. Not one to stay silent, that one."

Still, it didn't change the situation. Unless something happened, Eduardo was leaving right after Christmas. She dreaded the thought. She and Eduardo had struck up a rhythm of friendly antagonism and it always made the eighteen-hour day go by faster.

"Now, you be nice to this little girl," Miss Joan instructed, raising her voice so that the cook could hear her. "Don't be scaring her off. With you deserting me, I'm going to be needing someone to do the cooking. She can probably cook rings around you without even half trying," she predicted.

"She had better do much more than that if she is to survive here with you, old woman."

For a moment, as the swinging doors closed behind her, Angel thought of turning right around and vacating the relatively small, utilitarian kitchen. But something held her fast and wouldn't allow her to flee.

Was that "something" a basic part of her real makeup, or…

*Or what?* a voice in her head asked.

She had no answer for that, any more than she had an answer for any of the other dozen and a half questions that had assaulted her this past day and a half.

Eduardo's dark brown eyes looked her up and down slowly, his shaggy graying eyebrows drawing together little by little.

"So," he finally said, "you are here to take my place?"

"No, sir," Angel replied quietly and respectfully. "I'm just here to see if I can help out."

A small, almost nonexistent smile settled on Eduardo's thin lips and he nodded his approval at her choice of words.

"All right, then, come and help," he instructed. "You will find an apron in there," he added, nodding toward the small closet where towels, aprons and a host of other kitchen-oriented things coexisted in a jumbled heap.

Angel went to help herself to an apron. There was no denying that there were colliding butterflies in her stomach, but all the same, she *did* have a good feeling about this.

"Don't look so worried," Miss Joan chided Gabe as he watched the kitchen's swinging doors close behind Angel. "She'll be just fine. Eduardo hasn't required a human sacrifice since his third wife had the good sense to leave him."

"I heard that, old woman!" Eduardo called out. "And it is I who left her, not she who left me," the cook corrected.

"Whatever helps you get through the night," Miss Joan allowed with a dismissive shrug. "She left him," the older woman whispered to Gabe just before she accompanied him to the diner's exit. "Eduardo makes a lot of noise, but your little friend's going to be just fine," she reassured the new deputy.

Gabe started to issue a disclaimer that Angel wasn't "his little friend," but the truth of it was, he was stuck for an alternate label to apply to the woman he'd rescued yesterday. If Angel wasn't his "little friend"—and she *was* petite—how did he refer to her? As his project? As his work in progress? Or maybe just a lost woman?

Stumped, Gabe opted to leave the initial label alone until he could come up with a better one to take its place.

He supposed he should be grateful that Miss Joan hadn't referred to Angel as his new "girlfriend." Aside from that being totally inaccurate, it would have also been awkward for both of them if Angel had heard Miss Joan calling her that.

Weighing the two options, he came to the conclusion that "little friend" was definitely the lesser problematic of the two.

HEARING HIM ENTER, Alma glanced up from her computer.

"Where's your friend?" she asked. Craning her neck, Alma looked to see if he was indeed alone. "Her memory come back?" she asked.

"I left her with Miss Joan." He saw Alma's eyebrows rise in a silent question. "Turns out she knows how to cook really well."

"You made her cook for you?" Alma asked in amazement.

Gabe took exception to the implication. "I didn't

*make* her do anything. When I woke up this morning, she was making breakfast in the kitchen."

"In the kitchen," Alma repeated, the full impact of what he was saying finally hitting her.

"Yes," he answered, bracing himself for what he assumed was going to be another round of interrogation.

"And just what did she 'make' in your house last night?" Alma asked.

He knew exactly what she was asking and he wasn't about to get caught up in being defensive. He'd played that game before.

"We've already gone through this last night, remember? Get your mind out of the gutter, little sister, and make yourself useful," he told her. Nodding toward Alma's computer screen, he asked pointedly, "Did you find anything on her yet?"

She'd told him that she was going to go through the missing-persons reports. "So far, no," she answered. "Nobody's filed a missing-persons report looking for anyone who even vaguely matches Angel's description. But that's just in this county," she added. She spared a dark look toward her computer. "I'm going to widen the search as soon as the computer comes back to life."

Puzzled, Gabe looked at the screen. "Back to life?" he echoed. "What do you mean? The computer looks all right to me."

"Look closer," she urged, moving her chair to the side to allow her brother better access to her computer. "Try moving the cursor," she suggested.

When Gabe took possession of the mouse and moved it around on the desk, nothing happened. He had the exact same results hitting various keys on the keyboard. The last couple of keys he all but sank into the keyboard. Still nothing.

Alma physically removed his hands from her keyboard and pushed them to the side. "I think you get the picture," she told him.

Gabe's frown went down to the bone. "How long has it been like this?" he asked.

"For approximately the past ninety minutes. I actually came in early to get to work on finding our mystery woman's identity. What a waste *that* was," she complained.

"What did you do to it?" he asked.

"I didn't do *anything* to it," she retorted. "And for your information, the other computers have the same problem. As near as I can figure it, the system's been hacked into and infected with a virus."

Unlike the men in the office, Alma knew her way around computers and was, in effect, the one everyone turned to whenever they had any sort of a computer problem or question. But this seemed to require specialized expertise, not hit-and-miss tactics.

"So what are you doing?" he asked, gesturing at the immobile computer screen. "Just waiting for it to come back to life?"

"I've got a call in to the software tech support people, but I have a feeling it might be a while before they get back to us. In the meantime—" she shifted her chair around and reached for a thick folder on her desk "—I'm resorting to the old-fashioned method of looking through old reports manually to see if I can come up with any sort of a lead." With a smile, she added, "That comes under the 'no stone left unturned' heading."

Turning away from the confounding computer, she looked at her brother. "You didn't answer my question. Did Angel remember anything?"

He recalled the way the woman had worded it. "That cooking relaxes her."

"Let me rephrase that. Did she remember anything *useful?*"

"Like her name, rank and serial number?" Gabe guessed, clearly frustrated by the negative answer he had to give her. "No."

"You know, when this thing finally comes back from the dead—" she delivered less than a gentle tap to the side of the computer "—we could try taking Angel's fingerprints and see if we can come up with a name that way."

He was less than pleased about the implication behind his sister's suggestion. "You mean see if she has a criminal record?"

Alma looked more closely at her brother as she said, "No, I was thinking more along the lines of a driver's license, but hey, if you think there's a criminal record out there with her picture on it—"

"I don't," he snapped, cutting her off before she could continue down this path.

"Okay, then we'll look through the state's DMV records," she said, keeping her voice low-keyed. "Or maybe we'll get lucky and find out that our mystery woman works for the government, or that she served in the armed forces or the reserves at one point." She flashed her brother an encouraging smile. "It's going to take a while," she predicted. "But we'll find out who she is."

"She may not *want* us to find out who she is."

The latter speculation had come from Joe Lone Wolf. The deputy had apparently slipped soundlessly into the seat behind his desk while she and Gabe were discussing the best way to find out Angel's real name.

Caught off guard, Alma's hand instantly covered her heart as if to keep it from jumping out of her chest. "You know, you could try making a little noise once in a while, Joe," Alma complained. "Let people know that you're there."

His expression remained exactly the same as he said, "I thought I just was."

"I think I'm going to tie a bell around your neck," Alma threatened.

But Gabe's mind was on what Joe had said last. "Why wouldn't she want us to know who she was?" Gabe asked.

"A lot of reasons to try to lose yourself," the deputy answered matter-of-factly. In the world he came from— the reservation where he'd spent the formative years of his life—there'd been a lot of people who preferred making their way through life unnoticed. "Maybe she did something and she's on the run."

"I don't think—" Gabe began, ready to defend the woman.

"Not exactly hard, faking amnesia," Joe pointed out, cutting Gabe off. "There're no scientific tests around to use in order to prove that a person does, or doesn't, have amnesia."

"She's not faking it," Gabe insisted.

"And you know this how?" Joe challenged, willing to be convinced.

To back up his point, Gabe told them what happened last night. "She had a nightmare and she woke up screaming. There was this terrified look in her eyes." Gabe paused, knowing that he couldn't find the right words to express the feeling he'd had when he'd looked into her eyes. He *knew* she was on the level. Nothing could convince him that she wasn't.

"You had to have been there," he finally conceded with a sigh. "But I'd bet a month's salary that she's on the level."

"Last of the big-time spenders," Alma quipped affectionately. When her brother rose to his feet, Alma put her hand out to keep him where he was. "Relax, Gabe, I believe you." She looked at Joe pointedly. "So does Joe."

"Yeah," Joe chimed in after a beat. He'd sounded more convincing this time, but then there was never a great deal of feeling infused in Joe's tone, so Gabe let it slide. He didn't feel like getting into an extended, heated argument about that now.

"So what are you going to do if Angel *doesn't* remember anything more than how to deftly handle a frying pan?" Alma asked her brother.

He looked surprised at the question. "Me?" he asked. "Why me?"

Alma looked at him. "Because you seem to have appointed yourself her guardian angel, taking her under your wing so to speak." Light chocolate-colored eyes met dark. "Taking her home," Alma added, lowering her voice but keeping just the tiniest hint of emphasis evident in her tone.

Gabe knew damn well where his sister was trying to go with this. She thought he saw a substitute for Erica in Angel. She *couldn't* have been more wrong.

"The house has got three bedrooms, Alma," he reminded her.

"Yes, but only one bed," she countered.

"Which I let her have," Gabe immediately retorted pointedly.

"Ah, always the gentleman," Alma rhapsodized. "Relax, big brother, I'm just teasing you. Personally, I'm glad you've taken such an interest in her."

"I've taken an interest *in her case*," he emphasized. "An interest in helping her find her identity. I'm *not* interested in her personally," Gabe insisted.

"So, you can separate the two just like that, can you?" Joe asked. He sounded skeptical.

Gabe turned around to look at the man. Wrapped up in bringing his point home with Alma, he'd forgotten that Joe was even there. "I liked you better when you weren't making a sound."

A smattering of a smile creased Joe's lips for a moment. "Just asking the obvious."

Most of the time, Rick left his office door open. In part as an invitation to his deputies, letting them know that they were free to enter at any time if they needed to ask him or share something with him. As a consequence, he could hear everything that was going on—whether he wanted to or not.

In his opinion, this back-and-forth thing about a young woman with no memory who fate had dropped on their doorstep had to stop. It wasn't leading anywhere but to a huge headache for him.

Rick stuck his head out of his office. "Isn't it about time one of you went on patrol so the good citizens of Forever can go on believing that they have an actual sheriff's department looking out for their well-being?"

Gabe didn't have to be told twice. He was immediately on his feet. He could use a break from Alma's inquisition and Joe's knowing look.

"I'll go," he volunteered, grabbing the hat he hardly ever wore. For form's sake, he always kept the hat close by just in case he ever needed to put it on for some reason. Most of the time, the tan Stetson just rode on the seat next to him.

"Say hi to Angel for us," Alma called after her brother as he walked out the door.

Gabe made no answer, he just kept walking. He figured it was better that way all around.

## Chapter Nine

Eduardo Rubio was polite, but cold and distant when Miss Joan brought the young woman with the light blond hair through the kitchen's swinging doors and introduced them to each other.

To prove his point that not just anyone had what it took to keep up with the fast-paced orders placed by the lunch crowd—or the dinner crowd for that matter—Eduardo deliberately hung back and gave free rein to the young woman whom his boss had put into *his* kitchen. He opened the industrial-size refrigerator and allowed her to look around, then pointed out the pantry in what was close to utter silence.

"You will find everything you need there," he concluded, never really elaborating on which "there" he was referring to.

That said, Eduardo waited for the chaos to begin, convinced that this small woman with the improbable name of "Angel" would go running from the diner as fast as she could within the half hour.

He was wrong.

In less than a half hour, the previous fixture in Miss Joan's diner discovered that not only could this pretty little interloper keep up, she did it with a style and grace he couldn't help but admire, turning out meals with a little something "extra." They even looked inviting and festive on the plate after she finished arranging them.

For his part, Eduardo had never concerned himself about appearances when it came to the meals he prepared in Miss Joan's diner or in his own home for that matter. The customers who came in at these peak hours were focused on just grabbing something edible and getting back to work. As long as they enjoyed the taste, nobody really seemed to care all that much about what it looked like on a dish.

But this young woman, he had to grudgingly admit to himself, filled the orders and each serving was a poem onto itself, a feast for the stomach *and* the eyes.

Even Eduardo couldn't help but notice.

Silently surrendering, he began to work alongside of her.

"Where did you work before you came here?" Gabe asked. Wherever it had been, they had to have had an excellent training program, he couldn't help thinking.

The feeling of well-being that had been growing within Angel for the past forty-three minutes—the feeling that she'd somehow "returned" to an area that was familiar to her, to someplace that she actually "belonged"—began to break up like so many soap bubbles above a sink full of soaking dishes.

Why did he have to ask her that?

If the short-order cook had asked her what went into making beef Stroganoff, she could have rattled it off from memory as if she was reading the recipe off a chalkboard. It just felt like second nature to her. Right now, she felt like a composite of a huge host of recipes, nothing more.

But the man had asked her something that she couldn't answer. Something that brought her situation home to her again—that she didn't *know* where home was. Or *who* represented home to her. She didn't know *anything,* she thought in frustration.

The short-order cook just asked for the most elementary answer to the most elementary of questions, and she had nothing to offer him.

Nothing to offer herself.

It stood to reason that she had to have learned what she was doing in this kitchen *somewhere*—most likely a restaurant or some catering business or maybe even a doting mother or aunt had seen to her training—but exactly where she'd learned all this was utterly beyond her scope of knowledge.

Suppressing a sigh, she told him the truth. "I don't know."

Eduardo looked at her, equally suspicious and confused. Was she having fun at his expense? Did she think he was some foolish old man to be disrespected this way?

"What do you mean, you do not know? Of course you know. Why is it a secret? Did you learn to do this in prison?" he demanded, plucking the most unlikely setting out of the air. It was absurd and he knew it because no one taught anyone something even remotely sensually appealing in prison kitchens. From what he'd heard, it was all very utilitarian. If inmates weren't poisoned, or made wretchedly sick by what they ate, that was considered a successful serving.

At a loss, wishing she could get used to this emptiness in her head, Angel raised her eyes to the man's face and shrugged helplessly. "Because I don't," she told him.

"What, were you abducted by funny little green men and taken to their spaceship where they taught you all this?" he jeered, gesturing around at her handiwork. He was growing extremely annoyed that she didn't think enough of him to share such an insignificant piece of information.

Angel sighed as she watched over three separate meals, one on the grill, two on the burners, all frying at the same time.

"It might as well have been for all I remember," Angel confessed, shifting her eyes to his again. The cook seemed angry. Did he think she was lying to him? She didn't want bad feelings between them. "I don't remember anything," she stressed. "Not my name. Not where I was three days ago. Not why I almost drove my car over the side of the ravine."

Eduardo's features softened as her words sank in. He looked at her as if seeing her for the first time. "You are *that* girl?" he asked, his inference clear. The story about the young woman Gabe had rescued from the car before it exploded into flames had practically been the exclusive topic of conversation at the diner yesterday.

"I am that girl," she replied, none too happily.

Eduardo nodded, as if that was all he needed to know. Rather than remain standing off to the side, cynically observing her and searching for fault, Eduardo took his place beside her again and began helping her fill the orders in earnest.

He was not above frequently sneaking looks to see what she was doing. Eduardo discovered that seventy was *not* too old to learn a new trick or two. Very quickly, the meals that he was preparing began to take on a different, less hurried, more appetizing appearance.

"How's it going in there?" Miss Joan called into the kitchen when the last of the orders were slid out onto the metal counter.

"Very well, thank you," Angel replied, pleased. She smiled at Eduardo as if he had been the one to teach her rather than the other way around.

"I'm not hearing my angry cook picking on you," Miss Joan said, lowering her voice a little as she came closer to the counter where pieces of paper with orders on them traded places with hot plates filled with hotter meals. "Did he give up and leave?"

"I am here, old woman. Why would I leave? You have not paid me for this week, and if I leave, you would keep the money I have earned," he complained. But when he looked at Angel, the hint of a smile took root. He approved of her, but he wasn't about to let Miss Joan know this.

"Just checking," Miss Joan replied, doing her best to hide the chuckle she felt welling up in her throat.

The old SOB was staying, she thought with no small relief.

GABE WASN'T SURE just what he expected to find when he finally allowed himself to swing by Miss Joan's diner while on street patrol. It had been several hours since he'd dropped Angel off with the older woman.

Miss Joan hadn't called him to come and collect Angel, so he was hopeful that all had gone well. If it had, that meant that he'd come up with a viable way for Angel to earn a living until such time as he managed to discover who she actually was.

A woman that beautiful couldn't just drop off the face of the earth without someone looking for her.

The computers were still down, not just in the sheriff's office, but at the library and at the tiny post office, as well. All the computers were victims of some virus, which meant that for today—if not longer—no progress in the search for Angel's real identity would be made.

If he was being honest with himself, that fact didn't exactly disturb him as much as he would have initially thought it would. He supposed that something about Angel drew him to her and made him really enjoy the process.

Gabe was fairly sure that once she remembered who she was—or someone turned up who was looking for her—Angel would leave Forever.

He was in no hurry to see that happen.

He'd always been the type who felt that each day was to be enjoyed for its own sake. And he was certainly enjoying this one even more than he had the last one.

He looked forward to the next one, as well.

And, as long as she was here, he could keep an eye on Angel. Keep her safe.

That was particularly important since Mick Henley had dropped his bombshell on them earlier at the sheriff's office.

"Got a minute, Sheriff?" Mick had asked in his monotone voice. It wouldn't matter if he was announcing the end of the world, or ordering a beer, his cadence was always the same.

Since the mechanic rarely left his comfort zone and had sought them out, Rick was instantly alert. "What's up, Mick?"

"Dunno if this'll mean anything to you, but I had to take that girl's car apart."

"And what did you find?" Gabe asked. It had to be something or why else would the mechanic be here?

Mick looked at the sheriff, then at each of the deputies before continuing. "Her brake lines were cut."

"But she came all this way in that car," Gabe protested.

"The brake lines were cut just enough to go out on her after she'd left her starting point pretty far behind her."

"Somebody wanted her dead," Gabe concluded, stunned.

"Now I know why I hired you to take Larry's place," Rick commented wryly.

"But why would someone want her dead?" Gabe pressed, worried. "And who?"

"That, Deputy Gabe," the sheriff said in a kidding tone, although he was dead serious, "is the two-million-dollar question. The sooner we get some answers to our questions, the sooner that young woman is safe," Rick told his deputies.

Which was why Gabe had volunteered to go on patrol and take a second turn through his town.

"So, HOW'S IT GOING?" Gabe asked Miss Joan, doing his best to sound laidback and relaxed as he walked into the diner around three that afternoon.

For once, Miss Joan dispensed with her perpetual dour expression. Instead, her mouth was curved in what passed for a smile in Miss Joan's case.

"It's going *real* well," the older woman informed him. "Why didn't you bring me this girl sooner?" she asked.

"Well, for one thing, Angel wasn't here sooner," Gabe pointed out.

Miss Joan laughed. She poured herself a cup of coffee and one for Gabe, as well. She placed both on the counter before Gabe.

"Just pulling your leg, boy. I know all about when and how she got here—also know what a big hero you turned out to be," she added.

Gabe merely waved her last words away the way he might a persistent gnat.

"Did what I had to. Didn't do anything anyone else wouldn't have," he added, then got to the real reason for his ducking into the diner instead of just driving past it in his patrol. "So how's she working out?"

"Working out?" Miss Joan echoed. "Hell, because you brought her to me, I can rest easy because I found Eduardo's replacement."

"Do not be so fast to resting and replacing me," Eduardo called out of the kitchen.

Momentarily forgetting about Gabe, Miss Joan turned her attention to Eduardo, the man she had singularly relied on all these years.

"Why?" she asked. "You told me you were retiring, Eduardo, remember? All that fishing you wanted to do."

Eduardo made a dismissive noise. "The fish are not going anywhere—and neither am I yet, old woman," he informed her. "I have much to teach this young woman before I go."

Miss Joan snorted. "Seems to me, it's the other way around, Eduardo. I don't remember *ever* seeing anything come out of your kitchen that looked half as good as what that little girl whipped up time after time today. All out of her head, all beautiful to look at."

*Just like Angel,* Gabe caught himself thinking.

"Then perhaps it is time you went to Pine Ridge hospital and had those failing eyes of your checked out," Eduardo forcefully "suggested."

"I see everything just fine," Miss Joan answered with finality. "Including just what's going on. Can't pull the wool over my eyes, Eduardo, so stop trying."

Only Gabe saw the grin on the finely lined face. Miss Joan winked broadly at him as she continued hassling the cook she couldn't do without.

She lowered her voice so that this part of the conversation was strictly between her and Gabe. "Angel's welcome to work here for as long as she wants," she told him.

Nodding, Gabe said, "Thanks," and then, satisfied that Angel was all right, he took his leave again.

"No," Miss Joan called after him. "Thank *you*," she countered with emphasis.

He merely grinned just before walking out.

GABE RETURNED TO the diner when his shift was over. He was there to pick up Angel, assuming that her shift ended around the same time his did. He'd never paid attention to the comings and goings of the diner's staff. All he knew was that Miss Joan and Eduardo, her sparring partner, opened together and closed together.

He was fairly confident that Miss Joan would cut Angel some slack, especially since this was Angel's first day on the job.

On his way over to the diner, he stopped to make a pickup just prior to pulling up in front of the silver eatery. At the last minute, he decided to leave what he'd picked up on the passenger's side in the truck for the time being.

No point in letting everyone else in Forever see and have a reason to rag on him.

Walking into the diner, he found the place to be fuller than the hour customarily warranted. But since Miss Joan's diner was considered an unofficial gathering place for friends out to kill time and couples who wanted somewhere to sit and gaze into each other's eyes, Gabe just thought some meeting or other had been declared.

It wasn't until he was almost at the counter—and paying closer attention—that he realized that if there *was* a club meeting, the club centered around Angel and its members were comprised of all men.

There had to be at least ten seated or standing around her now, either vying for her attention or just absorbing her presence.

Miss Joan was the first to see him approaching. Like a regal queen, she beckoned him over to her.

As it turned out, the counter was far less crowded on her end than it was where Angel was seated. The young woman's back was to him.

"Business hasn't been this good since...well, I don't remember when," Miss Joan confessed openly. "That girl of yours turned out to be a gold mine—not to mention a treasure."

Gabe was about to protest—again—that Angel was *not* his girl, but as he opened his mouth, he was somewhat less inclined to make the disclaimer in light of the group of men all focused on Angel.

Watching even for a second, Gabe felt something exceedingly territorial stirring within him. He wasn't accustomed to feeling that way and he wasn't quite sure how to shake off the feeling—or if he even wanted to.

So all he said was, "Glad it's working out for everyone," and left it at that.

At the sound of his voice, Angel immediately turned around. The smile that rose to her lips was nothing short of beatific.

"Gabe," she called out. Delight and relief—and perhaps something more—echoed in her voice. The next second, she was getting off the counter stool she'd been perched on and making her way over to him.

Gabe found himself not just captivated by the look

in her brilliant blue eyes but almost falling into their fathomless depths, as well.

He was going to need to watch himself. Otherwise, things that he didn't want to happen just might do exactly that.

Happen.

"I hear you did really well today," he told her as Angel approached. He looked around at the men surrounding her. They appeared to be closing ranks around Angel again despite the limited amount of space.

"Let her breathe, guys," he said to the men, his voice sounding authoritative and official. "The lady can't move with you crowding her like that."

"Looks to me like she's moving just fine," one of the ranch hands from the McIntyre ranch piped up in response. The expression on his face showed all the signs that he was completely smitten.

"Your opinion doesn't count here, Wylie," Gabe informed the man. "Now I'm not telling you again. Let the lady through." This time there wasn't even a hint of humor to be found in his voice.

After a tense moment or two, Wylie raised his hands in surrender and stepped back. "Don't want no trouble."

"Glad to hear that," Gabe said, taking hold of Angel's arm and leading her to the door.

"See you tomorrow, Angel," Miss Joan called out after her.

Angel glanced over her shoulder. Her smile very nearly went from ear to ear as she repeated the sentiment to Miss Joan. Then she looked at the man at her side as he held the door open for her. "That's all right with you, right?"

He liked that she asked, even though she didn't have to. "You're your own person, Angel. I can't tell you what to do, but yes, for the record, that's fine with me. Miss Joan told me you did really well today."

Happiness seemed to emanate from her every pore. "It just seemed so right to me, to be doing what I was doing," she told him with enthusiasm.

He opened the passenger's side door for her and she was about to slide onto the seat when she stopped and looked up at him quizzically. "What's this?"

"Flowers," he answered matter-of-factly.

Holding the bouquet as if it was something fragile and precious, she slid into the passenger seat. "I know they're flowers, but why are they in your truck?"

Gabe got in on his side. Putting the key into the ignition, he left it idle for a moment as he turned toward her.

"Because I thought that maybe you'd like something to commemorate your first day at work." He shrugged, feeling oddly awkward about what he'd done on a whim. "Seemed like a good idea at the time," he murmured.

Angel inhaled deeply, the scent of roses both soothing and arousing her at the same time.

"It's a lovely idea," she told him.

Impulsively, she leaned over the stick shift and brushed her lips against Gabe's cheek.

Or would have had he not picked that moment to turn his head to look at her.

A cheek was replaced by a pair of lips. And what had been begun as the most innocent displays of gratitude escalated into something far more electrifying as her lips touched his.

Once.

Twice.

And then again a third time, each pass becoming just a little more forceful, a little more arousing than the last, until the bouquet fell from her fingers into her lap. Without thinking, Angel slipped her hands around the back of his neck.

Arms enfolded her, then Gabe pulled her closer to him and, just like that, completely lost his way.

## Chapter Ten

She could feel her heart hammering wildly in her chest. Angel was swept away by the sheer power of the emotion that had, without any warning, been unleashed full blown, within her.

All sorts of delicious sensations—new and yet not—raced through her, taking away her breath and making her pulse pound even more rapidly. She could feel her body reacting, could feel heat surging through her. Something vague, just out of reach, was trying—and failing—to break through.

It made her want.

It made her afraid.

Damn it, he had better control than this, a far-off voice in Gabe's head upbraided him. It wasn't as if Angel actually *knew* what was going on, or was making a conscious choice between refraining and giving in to a sudden impulse.

Hell, she might not even *know* what this impulse was at this point. Who could actually say—including her—what Angel knew and didn't know? Which meant that what he was doing right now was tantamount to plain taking advantage of her.

He should just pull back.

He should just stop…

But, oh, God, she was doing such things to his insides, reminding him what it felt like to be *alive*.

After Erica had ripped him to shreds, running over his soul with the equivalent of emotional cleats, Gabe had been fairly certain that he wasn't capable of reacting to another woman to any satisfactory degree. Not anymore. He'd even begun to make his peace with that. The way he saw it, he needed time to heal.

And if he didn't completely heal, if he remained on emotional lockdown, well, that was all right, too. The pain he'd gone through after the breakup was too huge to risk feeling again, anyway.

Which made what he was experiencing right now come as one hell of a shock to his system.

If they had been anywhere but in the front seat of his truck, front and center right before Miss Joan's diner…

But luckily for Angel—and maybe for him, too— they *were* front and center right before Miss Joan's diner, where any second someone could walk by, coming or going, and see them. He was *not* about to compromise Angel because his hormones had come back online or, for that matter, do anything that might reflect badly on the office of the county sheriff.

So, with a great deal of reluctance, Gabe took hold of Angel's shoulders and as gently as possible pushed her back, severing their almost-perfect physical connection.

Her breathing still a bit ragged, Angel looked up at him. The outline of her lips were blurred from the impact of his, and there was utter confusion in her blue eyes.

"Did I do something wrong?" she asked in a barely audible whisper.

"No. Oh, God, no," he added with emphasis, his voice growing in strength and feeling with each word. "I don't think I've ever felt anything quite so right in my whole life."

That brief, sizzling connection had sent everything soaring to record heights within him. It would be a while before it all settled down back into place. He tried to resist pulling her into his arms again.

Now she *really* didn't understand. "Then why did you stop?"

How did he begin to explain this? How did he tell her why he was obligated to stop something that his entire body was begging him to continue?

He took the easy way out. "We're in a very public place," he said.

As if to underscore his point, several people came out of the diner, passing his truck and absently looking in. They nodded as they made eye contact with Gabe.

"And you're ashamed to be seen with me?" Angel guessed. Otherwise, why had he all but pushed her away like that?

"No! Why would you even think that?" he asked, stunned she would suggest something like that. "I just don't want to compromise you."

How was making her feel warm and wanted possibly be compromising her? "I don't understand," she told him honestly.

Gabe started up the truck, still waiting for his own breathing to level off. He took his time answering her, hoping the words would fall into place. As he spoke, he deliberately avoided looking at her.

"You're vulnerable right now and vulnerable people do things that they wind up regretting later on." It sounded so stilted to his ears, but Gabe doubted he could explain it to her any better than that. Wanting her was interfering with his thought process.

She took a stab at making sense out of what Gabe was telling her. "You think I was kissing you for the wrong reasons."

It wasn't her kissing him that had him worried. It was where his kissing her was going to lead. But he wasn't really all that comfortable explaining the finer points of sexual attraction to her at this point.

So, for now, he took the way out she'd unknowingly offered. "Something like that."

"I wasn't," she insisted quietly. She wanted him to be clear on this. "I was kissing you for all the right ones. Because I'm grateful to you and because you make all these colors explode in my head." A soft smile on her lips, Angel looked at him, curiosity negating any residue embarrassment that she assumed she was supposed to be feeling—but wasn't. "Is this the way people feel when they're...attracted to someone?" she finally concluded.

She'd wanted to say "falling in love with someone" but she had a feeling saying that would make Gabe really back away from her. She didn't want that to happen, at least not before she had a chance to explore this delicious sensation that was all but taking root within her.

"That's part of it," Gabe allowed. Slanting a glance in her direction, he lowered his guard. As he did so, Gabe could feel himself beginning to smile. "Colors exploding, huh?"

"A whole rainbow's worth," she told him. "How about you?" she asked, her eyes on his face. "Seeing any colors?"

"No, no colors," he answered.

"Oh."

The lone word sounded incredibly sad as well as very isolated, he thought. For a second, he was tempted to come clean and tell her exactly what he really *was* feeling, but then decided against it. It would be better for her all around if she didn't know just how much she was affecting him.

He deliberately changed the subject. "So tell me about your day," he coaxed.

It took a beat, but then he saw Angel's face light up as she started to fill him in on how she'd fared in Miss Joan's kitchen with Eduardo.

When she finished, he was impressed and completely convinced that in all likelihood Angel could probably get along with the devil himself if need be. And if her narrative was any example, she would probably be able to find some kind of redeeming qualities about the fallen angel and list them in glowing terms.

She was, at this point, truly one of a kind. He wondered if that would change once her memory returned. He almost didn't want to find out.

"CHRISTMAS?" ANGEL repeated.

It was a little more than a week later—a week filled with a measure of self-restraint Gabe never thought he was capable of displaying—and he set the groundwork to tell her about the town's biggest holiday tradition.

"Christmas," he acknowledged, then suddenly paused as a thought hit him. Though he was beginning to piece a few things together, he still wasn't clear on the extent of what she knew and didn't know. "You do know what that is, right?"

She smiled tolerantly at him. "Yes, I know what Christmas is. My brain is missing some very crucial information, but it wasn't completely sucked dry or flattened to a pancake by the accident. I do remember some things."

*Just not who I am.* Although there had been dreams, dreams that vanished when she opened her eyes, but that brought with them a vague feeling of familiarity while they lasted.

"Just checking," he told her with a grin. "Anyway, everyone is getting together in the town square this afternoon to watch the annual Christmas tree being put up. It's being brought in sometime this morning—"

"From where?" she wanted to know.

"There's this forest north of here. We've been getting the town's tree from there for as long as I can remember. Anyway—"

She wasn't finished asking questions. "Who gets to pick the tree?"

Another question that had never occurred to him to ask. He'd just took what he'd observed as a given.

"Miss Joan usually goes along with whoever winds up bringing the tree back, so I guess, knowing Miss Joan, she does."

She nodded, accepting his explanation. "Could we go along, too?" She asked the question with all the eagerness of a child.

That would have been a case of too many cooks spoiling whatever it was that cooks conferred over, he thought, unable to remember the last of the old saying.

"*We* have work to do," he reminded her gently. It struck him how very domestic that line sounded to his ear. Like what a husband—or wife—might say to their spouse.

The thought did not spook him the way it might have once. As a matter of fact, this past week with Angel had played like a scene right out of that same fantasy, he couldn't help thinking. They went off to work together in the morning and he dropped her off at Miss Joan's diner, then stopped by there for lunch. And after his shift was over, he picked her up and they'd go home together.

To *his* house, not *their* house, Gabe emphasized pointedly. He had to remember to keep that in perspective. Once her memory returned—and more and more of him was beginning to really hope that either it wouldn't, or that that day was really far in the future—she, whoever *she* was, would leave and go back to her life.

And he would go back to the emptiness of his.

Empty in comparison to the way it was now, he deliberately specified for himself. Because right now, his life was filled with her chatter, her spontaneous laughter and her incredible cooking. Not to mention her warmth.

And because of that, Gabe was finding it harder and harder to restrain himself. Restraining himself when what he desperately wanted to do was sweep her into his arms and revisit the pulse-accelerating experience of kissing her.

Being alone with her—as pleasurable as it was— only seemed to insure that someday very soon he would find himself stepping over the line…hell, *racing* over the line, and making love with her.

To avoid that, he forced himself to have as little time alone with her as possible. And, with Christmas approaching, he'd come up with the perfect, albeit temporary way to be with Angel, but not *alone* with Angel.

"Because the tree is usually anywhere between eighteen and twenty feet tall, almost everyone in town turns out to help with the decorating," he explained, doing his best not to get lost in those upturned, wide blue eyes of hers. "I thought, while you were still here, you might want to join in."

There wasn't as much as a fraction of a second's hesitation. A wide smile curved Angel's mouth, spreading out, up to her eyes.

"I'd love to!" she declared enthusiastically. Swept up in the moment, she threw her arms around his neck, kissing Gabe.

Angel loved connecting with these people who had taken her in and offered her their friendship. Loved the idea of taking part in what the townspeople regarded as their tradition. Just as she loved working in the diner and listening to snippets of conversations around her.

Angel had taken it upon herself to learn as many of the customers' names as possible. She'd already learned the names of everyone who worked at Miss Joan's. Doing so gave her a warm sense of belonging. Something she sensed—without being able to offer herself any real proof—she hadn't really felt before.

Whether that meant that her "previous" personality was such that she had shied away from people, or that she had lived in isolating circumstances, she didn't know. All Angel knew—or rather sensed—was that this was different from the life she'd had before.

Different and preferable.

For just a split second, he almost gave in. Almost kissed her the way he so desperately wanted to kiss her. But he knew where that would lead and they both had places to be. And people who would ask questions if they didn't turn up.

So, digging deep for what might have been just the last of his resolve, he disengaged himself from her arms, gently placing them at her sides.

"All right, then," Gabe said as cheerfully as he could manage with his heart beating triple-time in his throat. "I'll stop by the diner around two and we'll go to the town square together."

She would have gone anywhere with him, including to the edge of the earth and beyond. But she had a sense of responsibility, especially to the woman who had given her a chance to explore this side of her that had flowered unexpectedly. "But I can't. I'll be at the diner, working, at two."

He shook his head. "Trust me. Nobody will be working at two today—at least, not at their regular jobs." He paused for a minute to take something out of the hall closet. "Practically everyone will be out in the town square, offering advice and encouragement, while a few poor souls struggle with widgets and a crane, trying to get the tree upright."

"Great. I'm game," she told him.

He caught her arm as she started heading for the front door. "Wait."

"Okay." A shiver of anticipation danced through her as she turned around. But before she could ask him what she was supposed to be waiting for, he thrust the shopping bag at her.

"I thought you might need this," he mumbled.

"'This'?" she repeated uncertainly. Looking into the bag, she was surprised to see what appeared to be a suede sleeve. The sleeve was attached to a jacket. A tan suede jacket with fringes that ran along the length of each sleeve and were also along the bottom of the jacket. She held it up against her. "Gabe?" she questioned uncertainly.

"Temperature's dropping," he told her. "Don't want you turning into an icicle." Although he couldn't help thinking there were other ways to keep her warm. Not exactly practical ways, but ways all the same.

"It's beautiful," she cried, quickly opening up the buttons.

Angel slipped the jacket on over the sweater she'd

been wearing. That, too, had been a gift, but from his sister, Alma. Up to this point, all her clothes had been gifts. Alma and she had turned out to be the same size and on the second day she was here, Alma had come over to Gabe's house with a large box of clothing she'd told her were just "lying around, gathering dust." The jeans, pullovers, everything that Alma had given her comprised her entire wardrobe.

Right now, Angel was torn between feeling like an ongoing charity case and very, very blessed. Knowing the spirit that this was intended, she focused only on the latter.

"Thank you. I really don't know how I'm going to be able to pay you back for all this—for the jacket, the food, taking me in," she elaborated. "But I am going to do my damnedest to try," she promised.

Moved by gratitude—just as she had been the first time—Angel kissed him. But the first time had been partially an accident. This time, she brushed her lips against his deliberately. And lightly. Anything else might have raised problems of varying degrees.

So this time, she was the one who drew back first. "We'd better go," she told him softly. "Before we're late," she added.

Damn it, he had to stop staring at her mouth like that when she talked, Gabe admonished himself. It was as if he was deliberately trying to sabotage his efforts to keep her at arm's length.

She was just here until someone recognized her or her memory came back. In either case, he had to remember that she was only passing through his life. A man couldn't let himself fall in love with someone who was just passing through. That would definitely be asking for trouble, not to mention heartache the magnitude that defied measurement, even on a Richter scale.

Still, a hundred times a day—not just today—he felt like giving in. Felt like giving himself permission to kiss her just one more time.

But he knew there was no "just" about it. If he relaxed his guard instead of maintaining it as vigilantly as he had been, there was no telling what would happen.

Or maybe there was, he amended, slanting a quick, stolen glance at Angel.

With quick, deliberate steps, he hustled out of the house ahead of Angel, then waited for her to follow so that he could lock the door.

Not that he had anything of importance to protect even if someone *did* invade his house. No, the thing in his house that needed protecting was walking ahead of him to his truck.

"THE MORE HANDS the better," Miss Joan declared later that day. It was two o'clock and, right on the dot, Miss Joan and the "Christmas tree hunting party" had returned with their prize.

Her words were addressed to Angel when the latter told her that she wanted to help with decorating the town's tree.

"You're going to be helping out, too, right?" Miss Joan asked, pinning Gabe with a look.

The question was a mere formality, since Miss Joan

expected everyone to join in, *especially* if she actually asked them to.

Gabe had briefly entertained the idea of begging off this one time. Doing so would give Angel some space and himself some breathing room. But he did enjoy this tradition, and even if he didn't, there was no arguing with the look on Miss Joan's face. What Miss Joan wanted, she got. Almost anyone in town could tell him that—if he hadn't known that for himself.

She'd never bothered asking him before, just assumed that he—like everyone else—would be there. That she actually had asked him made him think that either he was allowing his feelings for Angel to show, or Miss Joan was reading his mind.

Being that this was Miss Joan, it was most likely the latter, he decided.

In either case, he had to admit to himself that he was relieved that the decision was no longer his to make. To turn Miss Joan down was plain asking for trouble and he already had more trouble than he needed.

"Right," he replied, flashing a grin at the owner of the diner. "Wouldn't miss it for the world," he added for good measure.

"Good to hear," Miss Joan said with a nod.

Then, as her husband came to join her, the woman stepped back. With her fingers laced through his, she watched in rapt attention as the men she had accompanied on the "tree hunt" slowly righted Forever's latest Christmas tree.

She cheered and applauded as enthusiastically as everyone else once the tree was up and secured into place.

"Never get tired of seeing that," she confided. When she saw Harry looking at her, grinning, she cried, "What?"

"Like seeing you all caught up in this," he told her. "Makes me think of what you had to have been like, as a young girl."

"I was skinnier," she retorted dismissively. "C'mon, c'mon, grab some decorations," she urged her husband as well as Angel and Gabe. "We've got a lot of work cut out for us and the sun's not going to hang around, waiting for us to get done. Time's a-wasting," she declared, clapping her hands together, as if that would get everyone working faster.

Because it was Miss Joan doing the clapping, it did.

## Chapter Eleven

For a moment, when he pulled up to his house, Gabe experienced a feeling of déjà vu.

He thought that he was going to have to carry Angel into his house the way he had that first evening he'd brought her home.

His mouth curved as he vividly recalled that evening. At the time, it had seemed the simplest thing to do: bring the beautiful amnesia victim into his house just for the night and decide what to do about the situation in the morning.

Except somehow, that decision was reached.

Never explored.

Somehow or other, as one day fed into another, there were so many other things to deal with that finding another place for Angel didn't come up.

Seeing her like this now, sitting in the passenger seat, her head against the headrest, her eyes closed, stirred up all sorts of things within him: nostalgia, desire and a host of other feelings he knew he wasn't free to act upon.

Automatically slipping his key into his pocket the moment he turned off the engine, Gabe was about to get out of the truck and come around to her side when he heard her ask, "When are you getting your tree?"

With a self-deprecating laugh, Gabe settled back in his seat for a second and looked at her. Her eyes were open, which meant she wasn't talking in her sleep. "I thought you were asleep."

"Just resting my eyes," she told him.

That wasn't exactly the whole truth. She'd fallen asleep for a minute or two, lulled by the sway of the vehicle and the long day she'd just put in. But she'd woken up the second he'd brought his truck to a stop before his house.

"You didn't answer my question," she pointed out. "When are you getting your tree?"

"I wasn't really planning on it," he confessed. "My dad always has a really tall tree in his living room that we all help decorate, and, knowing Alma, she'll have one at her place, too. I didn't see the need to get a tree for my house, especially since it was just going to be me. All that work for just one person seemed like a waste to me."

"Not that I agree with you, but even so, it's not just you anymore," she reminded him, her eyes holding his prisoner. "Unless you want me to leave."

"No!" he cried, uttering the single word with a great deal more feeling than he'd intended. "No," he repeated, clearing his throat and sounding a lot more subdued this time around.

He didn't want her to think he'd prevent her from leaving—if that was what she wanted. But neither did he want her to think he was holding his breath, just waiting for her to leave.

"Of course I don't want you to leave. I guess that with everything that's been going on—trying to find out who you are, looking for a missing-persons file on you—I haven't been thinking beyond the moment." He shrugged now, trying to seem open to either decision. "Sure, we can get a tree if you'd like."

"When?" she asked with far more eager enthusiasm than he'd thought she was capable of right now, given that she'd done a great deal of climbing up and down the ladder, hanging decorations while balancing herself at precarious angles.

Well, it was much too late to go cut one down now, he thought.

"Tomorrow, I guess. Why? You didn't get enough of decorating today?" he teased. Her eyes, he noticed, were sparkling like a child's anticipating a meeting with Santa Claus himself.

"Never enough," she enthused. "I was kind of sorry when Miss Joan declared the tree done," she confided. "We could have at least put more tinsel on it."

Gabe laughed and shook his head as he got out of the truck, walked to her side and held the door open. "Any more tinsel and that tree was liable to fall over."

Without thinking, he slipped his arm around her shoulders, momentarily indulging in a one-arm hug as they walked up to his door. "You're really one of a kind, Angel," he marveled. And then he paused just before opening the front door as a thought struck him. "Did decorating the tree remind you of anything?"

"You mean did it make me remember?" He nodded, watching her expression, searching for a glimmer that hinted she was trying to pin down even a fragment of a memory. He saw nothing. "Almost," she admitted. "But every time I tried to reach for it, for any of the half shadows that slip in and out of my head so fast, they're gone before I even realize they'd been there. I wind up with nothing," she told him, a deep sigh accompanying her words.

"Maybe you should stop trying," he advised, not for the first time.

He closed the door behind them at the same time that he turned on the closest light switch. The lightbulb above their heads popped as the filament sent a surge of electricity through it. Just like that, darkness reclaimed the house.

"Don't move," Gabe instructed. "I'll turn on the next light."

Feeling his way around, he tried to make his way to the light switch leading into the family room. Instead, he managed to find his way to Angel. His outstretched fingers came in contact with something soft and he instantly knew it was her.

Gabe pulled his hand back. "Sorry," he murmured.

"That's okay," she said, absolving him of any wrongdoing. "I'm not," he heard her whisper.

Frustrated, wanting her more than was good for either one of them, Gabe momentarily halted his search for the light switch.

"You know," he complained honestly, "you're really not making this any easier."

"Making what any easier?" she wanted to know.

Was it his imagination, or had she taken a step closer? "Keeping away from you."

"Do you really want to?" She asked the question so quietly, for a brief moment he thought that perhaps he'd just imagined it—or she was communicating with him via her thoughts rather than any spoken word.

He also could have sworn his throat was tightening. "I think you know the answer to that."

"Tell me," she coaxed, her voice a sultry whisper.

He tried to steel himself—and failed. "No, I don't *really* want to."

"Then why?"

The words were softly whispered against his ear. He had to consciously struggle against giving in to the shiver.

"Because it's not fair to you," he told her. "You're dealing with a lot here, trying to remember your life before November 26 is just part of it. If I let my guard down," he said, thinking of all that entailed, all that would result from that simple act of omission, "and then somewhere down the line, you remember that there's another man in your life who you promised to love to the end of your days—"

"There isn't," she told him.

She said it with such finality, he almost believed her. He *wanted* to believe her. But, given her circumstances, he had to challenge her words. "You have amnesia. How can you say that with such certainty?" he added.

"I don't know," she admitted freely, "I just can. It's a feeling more than anything else. I wasn't married in that life I can't remember," she told him, confident that she was right. "It's nothing I can prove, it's just something that I *know*."

As she spoke, she drew closer to him until she was so close he could feel each breath she took as her chest rose, brushing against his. When she exhaled, he felt her breath along his skin.

His gut tightened in response as he struggled to hold himself in check.

He wanted to believe her. Wanted so badly just to take her into his arms, to make love with her and not fear the ramifications and consequences that were waiting for them just beyond the night.

But there *would* be ramifications and there *would* be consequences.

Gabe gave it one more try. "I need to find the light, Angel."

"It's right here," she whispered to him. He could feel her rise up on her toes, could feel her mouth teasing his as she spoke. "Inside me. Can't you see it? You make me glow."

He could feel himself weakening rapidly. "Oh, damn, Angel, you could break a saint."

"I don't want a saint," Angel told him, her eyes never leaving his. "I want you."

Gabe groaned as he surrendered, fully aware that tomorrow there would be hell to pay and most likely a mountain of regrets. If not tomorrow, then somewhere down the line.

But tonight, there was only her, only him and this bonfire of desire burning between them.

Closing his arms around Angel, he pulled her tightly against him, the hard contours of his body finding solace in her soft curves. The next moment, he sealed his mouth to hers.

The darkness became their friend rather than something to try to banish or to hold at bay. It enveloped them as one kiss flowered into another and then another.

And with each kiss, his desire for her grew. It grew at such a startlingly fast rate that he found he could hardly breathe. Wanting her consumed him, but he did what he could to hold himself in check. The last thing he wanted to do was frighten Angel because, Lord knew, feeling like this certainly managed to scare the hell out of him.

The rush he was experiencing was very nearly overpowering and stronger than anything he had ever encountered.

It was as if he had never desired a woman before, never wanted to make love with a woman to this degree before.

Never loved before.

The single four-letter word sliced at him, making him even more fearful.

And yet, short of the world coming to an end, he wouldn't have been able to stop himself from making love with her.

And maybe not even then.

ANGEL REALIZED THAT she was operating on pure instincts, following her body's urgings. Following them to a place she was utterly certain she had never been to before.

With every touch of his hand to her body, with every kiss exchanged, she felt her body heating a little more, felt desire consuming her a little more. Each pass took a little more out of her, propelled her a little further into this new, mysterious and wondrous place that Gabe had carved out for her.

For them.

As far as she knew, this was a completely new experience for her, one that, somewhere deep in her soul, she'd somehow known was waiting for her.

But only with this man.

Gabe had saved her life in more ways than one. In effect, he had *given* her her life, and everything she was or would ever be was because of him. In return for that, he'd asked her for nothing.

Which was why she'd given him her heart.

As desire fueled by eagerness continued to grow within her, she found that both her clothes and his began to disappear, vanishing in a haze and shed almost as quickly as any small, inconsequential inhibitions that might have been lingering.

She wanted Gabe to take her, to make her body sing. To make love with her until she all but sobbed with relief.

Angel arched into his touch, stifling a cry of pure ecstasy as she felt his lips pass over her body.

At least twice, if not more, she'd felt as if she was stepping out of her own body and watching everything unfold before her.

A spectator at her own field of joy.

It was incredible.

Her body ached for him as Gabe, murmuring endearments, led her to the bedroom and laid her on the bed, then slowly slid his body along hers again until he was level with her and his eyes were looking into her depths.

Anticipation roared through her veins.

"Now," she whispered hoarsely. "Now."

But when Gabe grasped her, ever so lightly, by her shoulders, a sense of panic suddenly barreled in out of nowhere and exploded within her.

He felt her instantly stiffening beneath him, heard the change in her breathing. It was rapid now, not from any sort of anticipation of pleasure but from direct fear. Exercising what was quite possibly the very greatest effort of restraint of his life, Gabe forced himself to stop, and drew back.

His eyes searched her face for a clue. Angel seemed terrified, he realized. Why? "What's wrong?"

"I can't breathe, I can't breathe," she cried. Without his weight—and his hands—restraining her, she bolted upright, dragging air into her lungs like a near-drowning victim.

Gabe's first instinct was to hold her in order to calm her, but he had a feeling that would only bring the opposite results. So he held himself in check until he could sort out exactly what had set her off and what was happening here.

He made the only logical assumption. "You remembered something, didn't you?"

"No!"

The denial was automatic, as if she'd been quizzed about her reaction more than once before and this was the answer she gave time and time again. It was, he had a feeling, the expected answer.

But for who?

Angel drew in more air, this time more slowly as she struggled to get hold of herself. After a beat, calmer, she looked up at him.

"Yes," she answered, bewildered and drained. Rocking, she locked her arms around herself. "He was forcing himself on me, holding my shoulders down so I wouldn't fight him off."

Angel's mouth dropped open. She seemed as startled by what she'd just said as Gabe was to hear it.

"Who?" Gabe asked, trying his best not to press her too hard. He wanted her to think, to remember, and he knew she couldn't if he cornered her. "Who was forcing himself on you, Angel?" he asked more gently.

"I don't know." The frustration was back, spilling out in her tears. "I don't know," she repeated. Angel closed her eyes, but there was nothing. Opening them again, she exhaled a shaky breath as she dragged her hand through her hair. "I can't see him, can't seem to make him out."

Very carefully, Gabe slipped his arm around her shoulders. But rather than pull away or resist him, she relaxed. He could feel her tension draining from her. Whatever had slashed through her moments ago had been leeched out, leaving her exhausted.

Angel leaned her head against his shoulder. "Why can't I remember, Gabe?" she demanded. "Or, if I can't remember, why can't I just forget about it completely?"

She hated being stuck like this, half in limbo, half out.

"Because you're a strong woman and you want to face whatever demons are secretly tormenting you. And you will," he promised, pressing a kiss to her forehead. "And when you do, I'll be right there, facing them with you. I'm not leaving you to deal with this alone."

She raised her head to look at him. He was making her a promise, she realized.

"I'm sorry," she murmured.

"Nothing to feel sorry about," he told her. "We don't have to do anything. We can just lie here together until you fall asleep."

"No," she said after a moment.

"You want me to go?" he asked.

Moved, she cupped her hand against his cheek, caressing it. Warm feelings stirred within her and grew warmer. "No, I want you to make love with me, Gabe," she said quietly.

He turned her hand palm side up and pressed a kiss to it. He heard her draw in a breath in renewed anticipation.

"Are you sure, Angel?" he asked. He didn't want to do anything that would bring back that frightened look he'd just seen.

"I'm sure," she told him with certainty. "Make the demons go away, Gabe."

She was asking a lot of him, but he wasn't going to fail her, he silently swore.

Drawing her back into his arms, he started making love to her very slowly, kissing only her lips until she all but melted against him. And then he widened his scope, anointing her throat, her shoulders, working his way down to the sensitive insides of her elbows.

Hearing her sigh as his own blood heated, he kissed one breast at a time until she was all but panting beneath him. Her pleasure was his aphrodisiac.

He trailed his lips along her belly. It quivered in response.

Angel twisted and turned against him, attempting to absorb every sensation, clinging to the ever-growing surge of desire. Catching her breath as each arrow of desire shot through her.

All the while, she was determined that the shadowy figure would be vanquished by this man she'd entrusted with her heart.

This time, when he came to her, Gabe deliberately switched their positions, gently guiding her hips until she was the one over him. She looked down at him with wonder and he smiled, silently coaxing her to take the lead. The exhilaration he saw in her eyes aroused him to a higher degree.

Driving himself into her, gently but forcefully, he could feel her arching against him, letting him know that she wanted this union as much as he did.

Locked in an embrace, their souls sealed to each other, they quickly built up the rhythm that would in turn usher them to the ultimate moment.

And when they reached it, when a shower of lights and sounds and feelings finally rained down on both of them, they clung to each other, each trusting the other to keep them safe and whole, and out of harm's way.

## Chapter Twelve

It took a while for the euphoria to fade into the darkness. When it did, and Angel still hadn't said a word, concern prompted Gabe to quietly ask her, "Are you all right?"

He heard a soft sigh escape and then she turned into him. There was a smile on her lips. "I'm perfect."

Gabe laughed. "I already know that. But I'm asking if—"

Angel didn't let him finish. She pressed her fingertips against his lips, not wanting to spoil the memory of the afterglow with questions about her temporary break from her present reality.

"Everything's fine. Better than fine," she added with feeling. Her eyes held his as she implored, "I don't want to talk about what happened earlier."

Ever so slightly, Gabe tightened his arm around her. "All right," he agreed, although they both knew that she would have to talk about it eventually. Talk about what had panicked her like that. They needed to solve the puzzle that had been her life before she came to Forever and this could have been a very important piece in that puzzle.

But that was for later. For now, he wanted her to

enjoy what they'd just shared. They both deserved a little happiness after everything they'd gone through in their lives before their paths had so abruptly crossed.

Not wanting her to feel that he was crowding her, Gabe began to get up.

Surprised, Angel caught his hand before he could leave the bed. "Where are you going?"

"To the sofa. I thought you might want your space," he explained.

Space was the last thing she required right now. Space allowed her to think and all she wanted to do was feel, not think.

"Stay with me," she said to him.

It was a request, not a plea, but either way, it wasn't in his power to refuse her. Lying down again, looking for a way to lighten the serious mood, he warned her, "I might hog the blankets."

In response, a smile curved her mouth. "I'll chance it," she said, curling up into him. "Besides, you're nice and warm. It's like having my very own fuzzy electric blanket."

To emphasis her point, she lightly stroked her fingertips along the downy hair on his chest. With a contented sigh, she laid her head on it, the sound of his heart beating beneath her ear giving her more than a little comfort.

"Fuzzy electric blanket, huh?" Humor curved his mouth. "First time anyone's ever called me that."

Her even breathing told him he was talking to her while she slept. Gabe wasn't certain why, but he found the thought immensely comforting.

"So? Have you decided yet?" Gabe asked Angel.

It was several days—several incredibly blissful, lovemaking days—later and he was finally getting the chance to make good on his promise to take her Christmas tree hunting.

While, in his opinion, Angel was in a class by herself in many, many ways, she now displayed a trait considered exceedingly common to the female of the species: she couldn't make up her mind. In this case, she was undecided between two trees.

Initially, there'd been five trees, five semifinalists she'd circled around slowly so she could see which of the trees had the most "good sides." Now that they were down to two, she was having a harder time finding one to eliminate.

"You're going to have to make up your mind before it gets dark," he told her. "Otherwise, we'll have to come back."

She noticed that he didn't say "tomorrow," which meant that he probably wouldn't be able to take any more time off for at least a few days. Which, in turn, meant a few more days without a tree and Christmas was drawing closer and closer.

She had to make up her mind *now*. But it was hard.

"I *have* narrowed it down to just a couple of them," she reminded him in her own defense. Vacillating, she made her way back to a small tree. Once cut down, she knew it would more than adequately fill the living room, the room.

"Angel…" Gabe's voice trailed off as he waited for her to finally choose.

The temperature was dropping and they were both getting colder. It was time to pick a winner. "Okay, okay, this one," she declared, choosing the tree closest to Gabe.

But as she came up to it, studying the tree intently, Angel cocked her head as if that gave her a different perspective. "Still..."

"No, no 'still,'" Gabe told her firmly, taking the first swing at the tree's trunk with his hatchet. "This is the tree you just picked and this is the tree that's coming home with us." There was no room for argument as he took a second swing and made contact again.

She threw her hands up in surrender. "Okay. You're right. This is the tree." And then she chewed on her bottom lip. He'd begun to realize that she did that whenever she was undecided and vacillating between choices. "It's just that, since this is your first Christmas tree in your new house, I wanted the tree to be perfect."

He took a third swing. "First off, the house *isn't* new—"

"It is to you," she pointed out as hatchet met tree again. Gabe had on a jacket, but she could just *see* his muscles rippling.

"And second," he continued, "there's no such thing as 'perfect.'"

Which was when Angel smiled up into his face. The look in her eyes caused his gut to all but seize up and do backflips.

"Yes, there is," she told him softly and pointedly— just before she brushed her lips against his.

And just as with the first time, Gabe found himself utterly captivated, unable to resist her.

Unable to resist the powerful need that sprang up within him. The need to take her into his arms and kiss her for all he was worth.

Releasing the hatchet, Gabe swept her into his arms and kissed her hard.

He was surprised by the force of the kiss that met him. Angel had not only returned his kiss, she damn well matched it.

Gabe could feel his body firing up, and for one dizzying moment he thought of giving in and making love with her right here, in the middle of the forest.

The next moment, the absurdity of the thought hit him. He was an adult, a representative of the law, for heaven's sake, not some sex-starved adolescent with his first girlfriend.

Drawing away, he laughed softly at himself, shaking his head. When had he reverted back to his adolescence? He might not have been the most clear thinking of men, but he'd always been aware of what he was doing, aware of how things might look to someone else. Recklessness was not part of his nature.

Until now.

Taking in a breath, he framed her face as he looked into it. Even such a small, innocent action stirred his heart.

"We keep going like this, we're going to wind up with hypothermia," he warned.

Taking in a deep breath, she waited until she released it again and had steadied herself just a little. Angel nodded as she glanced down at the ground. "Might make for an interesting snow angel—if there was snow on the ground," she commented.

"Speaking of which." Gabe pointed up to the sky with an amused laugh. As if on cue, the lightest of flurries had begun to descend. "Just how did you do that?" he teased.

Her eyes crinkled. "Wishful thinking."

He picked up the hatchet again. "Well, wish for it to continue being light until I finish cutting down your tree."

"Our tree," she corrected since it was going into his house and he was providing the elbow grease used to cut it down.

He took another swing, cutting away a little more of the trunk. "Our tree," he amended agreeably.

And, heaven help him, he really liked the sound of that. Liked the sound of the word *our.* This after he'd sworn off having anything to do with the so-called "softer" sex, other than serving and protecting them in his capacity as deputy sheriff.

Without firing so much as a single shot, this petite, vibrant woman had managed to capture him and take him prisoner.

The tree came down after a few more swings of his hatchet. Though he told her he could handle it, Angel insisted on helping him bind up the tree and, together, they got it up on the roof of his vehicle. He was surprised at how strong she turned out to be.

Gabe strapped the Scotch pine down as securely as he could and then they drove back to his house. He was careful to drive slowly, going at a speed that a lame turtle might have thought to be embarrassing. But it was necessary; otherwise, the wind might have wound up knocking off the tree or even taking his roof with it.

Consequently, it was pitch-black by the time they reached his house.

Easing the tree down from the roof, they then carried their prize into the house with Gabe doing his best to take on the brunt of the weight without letting her realize it.

Once they got the unwieldy tree inside, he thought about just leaving it lying on its side where it was, in the hallway. Tomorrow was plenty of time to place the tree upright in the stand that Angel had surprised him with.

But one look at Angel's face and he knew that waiting until tomorrow wasn't going to be an option. She was already moving around the living room, trying to decide where best to place the tree in order to show it off to its maximum advantage.

"Christmas trees don't have a 'maximum advantage,'" he told her, doing his best to hide his amusement. In a way, it was like watching a child preparing for Christmas for the first time.

He supposed, in a way, Angel actually was.

"Sure they do," Angel insisted. "Unlike fake ones, real Christmas trees are *not* the same from all angles." She lowered her voice a little, as if sharing a confidence with him. "Our tree has a couple of barren spots."

It was getting harder and harder not to laugh, but he didn't want her thinking he was laughing at her. "If you say so."

She looked at him, surprised. "Didn't you notice them?"

"Nope," he admitted freely. "I was too busy being completely dazzled by the angel standing beside me, issuing orders."

She shook her head. Now he was just pulling her leg. "Very funny."

She started to go to the kitchen to get some water for the base of the tree after they finally got it into the stand. Catching her by the elbow as she went by, Gabe pulled her into his arms.

"Not really," he told her. "Actually, it all seems very serious, at least to me." Holding her to him, he gave in to the urge that he'd been wrestling with all the way home. He kissed her. Then, as he drew back his head again, he shook it, utterly mystified. "What the hell have you done to me, Angel?" Affection laced every word. "What kind of spells do they teach you to cast in your world?"

She was incredibly content. *Too* content. And that worried her. She was afraid that something would happen to steal all of this away from her.

But for tonight, she'd pretend that this would go on forever and that this was paradise.

Because it was.

She threaded her arms around his neck, savoring the moment. Savoring him.

"The same kind they teach to cast in your world," she answered quietly just before she pressed her lips against his.

They got around to putting up the tree and decorating it a great deal later than Angel had initially anticipated.

The delay was well worth it.

DESPITE THE FACT that only small bits and pieces of her previous life started to fall into place—she had a preference for Mexican food and was able to create minor miracles in the kitchen—Angel found that she was less and less focused on trying to remember the life she'd had before coming to Forever.

That was largely because she was happy here, happy in a town that had accepted her so readily. And far more than just "happy" with the man who had come into her life, a man who continually placed her wants and needs above his own each and every time.

For all intents and purposes, she'd been a clean slate when Gabe had rescued her. As the days slipped into one another, she felt the desire to find her past lessened bit by bit. If she never found out who she was or why she'd wound up here, well, that was all right, too. As long as she was allowed to remain here, with Gabe, for the rest of her life.

She had an underlying fear of what any sort of "discovery" about her previous life would yield. Although she was inexplicably certain that she didn't have a husband waiting for her somewhere, Angel began to suspect that if she *did* remember all those pertinent pieces of information about herself and her world, she wouldn't be too happy with what that discovery would yield.

So, banking down what she assumed was a natural strain of curiosity, Angel stopped asking Gabe if he'd found out anything when she saw him at the end of each day.

Instead, she focused on the evening ahead, whether that involved just the two of them in his house, or visiting with his family, or just staying at Miss Joan's diner after her shift was over, enjoying the company of the people she'd come to think of as her friends.

"HARD TO IMAGINE what it was like without her around, isn't it?" Miss Joan commented to Gabe as Angel disappeared into the kitchen after volunteering to prepare dinner for one of her regular customers. The man had been unavoidably detained and looked genuinely disappointed when he realized he'd arrived too late for her to make his dinner. Taking off her jacket, Angel was quick to set his mind at rest as she headed back into the kitchen.

She'd been touched by the man's apparent disappointment so she'd told him to hang on and away she went to prepare his dinner, tossing a "you don't mind, do you, Gabe?" over her shoulder.

"No, I don't mind," he'd called after her, but he doubted if she'd heard.

How could he stop her? Her selflessness was one of the things that made Angel Angel. And it was one of the reasons why he'd fallen in love with her.

"Yeah," Gabe heard himself admit, answering Miss Joan's question.

And it was true. He'd gone from zealously guarding his feelings to allowing others to see just how caught up he was in this woman.

Damn, he'd sure come a long way from that man Erica had trampled. That man who, right after that, had sworn off any and all relationships for the next decade—if not longer.

"Making any headway finding out her real name?" Miss Joan asked. Her voice had a mildly disinterested ring to it, but she wasn't fooling him. The woman had ears like a bat and could listen to three different conversations at once. "The IT guy from County said he finally got rid of that virus that took all your systems down."

Gabe eyed the older woman. Everyone who lived in or passed through Forever wound up eating at the diner, and somewhere along the line they'd find themselves, quite unintentionally, baring their souls to Miss Joan. Gabe wasn't too surprised that the woman knew something that only he and the other deputies in the sheriff's office knew.

"Not yet," he told Miss Joan. "Up until now, Alma's been combing through the files by hand, placing calls to other sheriffs' offices and police stations. At first it was only within a hundred-mile radius, but then she expanded it somewhat when she didn't get a positive response."

He'd found out that his sister had made up a small poster with Angel's picture. She made sure it was mailed out to all the various offices.

The process was painfully slow in comparison to what they'd become accustomed to, but in lieu of a functioning computer—each would shut down the moment the internet was accessed—that method had to suffice.

Now, however, they had gotten back on track and things would move far more quickly again.

*If* there was anywhere to move, Gabe silently qualified.

On a personal level, though he knew it was selfish, he hoped that they would never find out who Angel actually was and where she belonged. She was *his* Angel and that was all that really mattered to him.

But, as one of Forever's deputies, he felt obligated to do whatever he could in order to get answers for Angel—or whatever her real name was.

As if reading his mind, Miss Joan leaned her head closer to his and suggested, "Why don't you let it go until after Christmas?"

Not that he wasn't sorely tempted, but that would be giving in to a personal whim. Gabe shook his head. "Wouldn't be right."

To which, in response, Miss Joan shrugged her thin shoulders. "Oh, I don't know. There's 'right,' and then there's *right*."

She walked away then, leaving him to contemplate the difference—and secretly wishing for the advent of another computer virus.

## Chapter Thirteen

The police detective froze as the image of the young woman on the bulletin board he'd just passed registered with his brain.

Stunned, he backtracked the few steps he'd taken and stared at the eight-by-ten photocopy secured onto the overfilled board with thumbtacks haphazardly stuck into two of its corners. The quality of the photograph wasn't the best, but it was good enough to stop the breath in his lungs.

That was *her,* it had to be.

But how *could* it be?

Dorothy was dead.

There were three small, concise paragraphs on the sheet directly below the photograph. The first time he scanned them, not a single word penetrated his brain. Banking down his mounting agitation, he read the paragraphs again. And then a third time. Finally the fog around his brain began to release its hold. He could make out the words.

The woman had been found in Forever, Texas. Whoever had sent out the poster was trying to find out who she was. Apparently the woman had been involved in an accident and had lost her memory.

*Yeah, right,* he silently jeered.

Anger, relief and disbelief all stampeded through him as he reread the words for yet a fourth time.

Maybe it was true. Maybe Dorothy had lost her memory. He turned the idea over in his head. That meant a clean slate, a clean start.

He smiled for the first time since the poster had caught his attention. If it was true, maybe this time she would get things right. There'd be no problems if she just got things right.

He could bring her home and start over.

A second chance.

He nodded to himself as he took down the poster. Maybe it would work out, after all.

Changing direction, he went in search of his lieutenant. He was going to need some time off to go down to Forever and bring her back.

Forever.

He laughed shortly under his breath. Had to be some little pimple of a town that undoubtedly housed a couple of hayseed families and a bar. He'd never heard of it before, but that didn't matter. He'd find it. And bring her back.

One way or another.

"She got you to get a Christmas tree, huh?" Alma asked her brother the second Gabe walked into the sheriff's office the next morning.

He was late and that wasn't like him. Ordinarily

she'd rag on him for that, but the Christmas tree purchase was just too good to pass up without a comment. That took front and center.

Gabe could see that his sister had been all but bursting, waiting to spring the subject on him. That was Alma, all right. He supposed he should count himself lucky that his sister hadn't called him in the middle of the night to laugh about the change he'd undergone since he'd saved Angel's life.

It seemed that by saving hers, he'd transformed his own.

He did his best to look as if he was scowling at his sister. He and Angel had gone directly home with the tree, not stopping to talk to anyone. How the hell did Alma find out?

"Who told you?" he asked.

"I have my sources," she informed him smugly.

"Mona saw you when she was coming home after paying Ed Sawyer's colicky mare a visit," Joe Lone Wolf told him matter-of-factly in his monotone voice. Gabe turned around to look at the sheriff's brother-in-law. Joe shrugged, as if the outcome had been predestined and inevitable. "She told me, I told Alma."

Gabe sighed. He should have known that nothing remained secret or private in Forever. Some things just took longer to get around than others. But they all got around eventually.

He shrugged as he sat down with the coffee he'd gotten at Miss Joan's when he'd dropped Angel off. It was still steaming.

"No big deal," he told his sister with an indifferent

shrug. Removing the lid, he tossed it into the wastebasket. He figured the coffee wasn't going to last him long enough to require being covered again.

"No big deal?" Alma echoed, getting up and crossing to his desk. "When I asked you at Thanksgiving if you needed any help in picking out a Christmas tree for your new place, you gave me a ten-minute speech about 'not needing any commercial trappings' to remind you what holiday to celebrate." Making no effort to suppress the grin on her lips, she pinned him down with a penetrating look. "As I recall, you were pretty adamant."

Gabe took a long sip of his coffee as he looked away. "So I changed my mind," he said with a touch of impatience. "It happens."

Alma's grin turned into an utterly enigmatic smile. "Yes, it seems that it certainly does."

"Don't make a big deal out of it," he warned her.

"Okay," Alma agreed. "No big deal." She pinned him with a look. "Does that mean you don't care if I got any responses to that poster of Angel I sent out?"

He hadn't thought he could switch from being seemingly casual to a man on tactical alert in under a second, but he could and he did.

"Did you?" he demanded sharply.

"Then you do care," Alma concluded.

"Alma, give me a straight answer to my question or so help me…"

When his voice trailed off, she jumped right in. "So help you what? Help you level with your sister?" Alma suggested.

Joe rose, unfolding his lanky torso. "I think I'll look

in on Ben, see how our resident town drunk is doing this morning," Joe said to no one in particular.

"See if he's sober and ready to go back to his wife," Alma called after Joe's departing back.

"It's either one or the other. If he's sober, he won't be ready to go back to his wife," Joe pointed out without turning around.

Turning back to her brother, she coaxed, "Why don't you just admit that Angel's gotten to you? After all, she's beautiful, bright, cooks up a storm and anyone with eyes can see that she's just crazy about you." Alma rested her case. "In short, she's everything I ever wanted for you."

"Fine, 'Mom.'" He deliberately inclined his head submissively, although he did manage to keep the sarcasm down. "She's gotten to me. Now answer the question. *Has anyone called about the poster?*"

Alma dropped her teasing attitude and shook her head.

"Not so far, no." She felt obligated to add a coda to that. "The posters probably got lost in the shuffle."

"Most people don't pay that much attention to something that comes via snail mail these days," the sheriff commented.

Brother and sister turned to look toward Rick's office. Their boss was standing outside the doorway, nursing what amounted to his third cup of hot tar.

"How long have you been standing there?" Alma asked.

Though Rick was generally affable, Alma was the only one in the office who ever challenged him or acted as if they were basically on the same level. She'd been with the sheriff's department the longest length of time and figured that put her on close to equal footing with Rick.

"Long enough to decide that there isn't a brother and sister on earth who don't argue," Rick replied, a half smile on his lips. "So, no takers for our amnesia victim?" he asked, looking to confirm what he'd overheard.

"None," she replied. "And I haven't found any matches to missing persons files since our system came back up yesterday," she added.

"Would be nice to tell 'Angel' who she really is by Christmas," Rick speculated.

Alma exchanged glances with her brother. "Maybe Angel doesn't want to know who she is," Alma suggested.

Had Angel said something to Alma? Gabe wondered. "What makes you say that?" he asked suspiciously.

Alma shrugged. "Just a gut feeling," she admitted. "I figure if it really mattered so much to her, she would have been pushing us to try harder."

"Meaning what?" Gabe asked. Was she suggesting that Angel wanted to cover something up?

"Down, Gabe. I meant no disrespect here. It's just that maybe, on some level, she's afraid that she won't want to find out who she is. Maybe, when you found her, she was already running from something."

Gabe had his own theories on that. He snorted. "Most likely whoever it was who left those fatal notches on her brake lines."

Rick nodded, agreeing. "Sounds like a good theory

to me. Too bad the sedan was so badly damaged. There might have been a decent set of prints or two we could have lifted."

Gabe nodded, but his mind had raced ahead and was now elsewhere. What if someone *did* recognize her from that photocopy Alma had sent out? How was he going to be able to determine that whoever came looking for Angel wasn't the guy who'd obviously set out to kill her?

He frowned. "Really wish you hadn't sent out that poster, Alma."

"We had to do something," she pointed out defensively. "Can't just hang back and let her go on wondering who she is for the rest of her life."

What Alma said was true enough on the surface, but what if what Angel found out was something she would have rather left buried in the recess of her mind? He'd be doing her no favors by digging all that up.

Just then, a loud noise erupted from the rear of the building where their jail cells were located. Stunned, all three law enforcement officers quickly made their way to the back where they discovered Ben Walker, the man known affectionately as one of Forever's two resident drunks, was standing on his cot, looking properly terrified by the slip of a woman standing on the other side of the cell's bars, shouting at him to stop acting like the state's biggest ass and the greatest disappointment of her life. The sentiment was reinforced and peppered with a great many blue words.

"Now, Eleanor, you know I'm going to have to fine you for all those cuss words coming out of that genteel mouth of yours," Rick told the woman mildly. Glancing toward his brother-in-law, he asked, "How much is Eleanor up to now, Joe?"

Joe paused for a second to calculate, then answered, "Twenty-five dollars by last count."

"Well, it's all worth it," Eleanor declared with a toss of her dyed flaming-red hair. "You'd cuss, too, if you had to be married to that poor excuse for a man," she informed the sheriff, gesturing dismissively at her husband.

Rick took hold of the woman's shoulders and looked into her eyes. "Eleanor, it's almost Christmas and in the spirit of the season, I'm going to forget about your fine—but I want you to practice a little of that Christian charity you're so famous for and give your husband another chance."

"Another chance?" she echoed incredulously. "I've already given him another chance. I've given him a *dozen* extra chances—"

"Then it shouldn't be all that hard to give him one more," Rick said amiably. There was resistance in the woman's rounded face. "Do it as a favor to the rest of us," he coaxed.

Eleanor Walker, who had at one point in time been considered to be quite stunning, sighed dramatically. Twice. And then she shrugged in surrender, mumbling, "All right, but only for you, Sheriff."

"Thank you, Eleanor. Can't ask for anything better than that." Rick looked pointedly at the man still standing on his cot, eyeing his wife fearfully. It made for a ludicrous scene, seeing as how Ben was twice his wife's size. "And you, Ben, I want you to promise not to touch a drop of anything with alcohol in it for the next thirty days—"

"Thirty days!" Eleanor cried, outraged that the time limit was so short.

"Thirty days?" Ben lamented at the same time. The expression on his face clearly indicating that he viewed thirty days to be close to an eternity.

"Thirty days," Rick repeated. "Otherwise, I'm locking you both up—in the same cell." Inserting his key in the lock of his prisoner's door, he looked from husband to wife, then back again, waiting. "So is it a deal?" he asked.

Having no choice, Ben nodded sheepishly. "It's a deal."

"Deal," his wife grumbled, spitting the four-letter word out.

Rick paid no attention to either tone, only to the promises that had been given. "That's what I like to hear," he told both parties as he pulled open the cell door.

Ben never took his eyes off his wife, watching her fearfully, as he exited the cell.

As the sheriff walked out with his deputies, his former prisoner and Ben's wife, he was surprised to find someone waiting for them in the office.

"Hi," Angel greeted them brightly. "I heard your voices so I let myself in. I hope you don't mind," she said to Rick.

"Not at all. Is there something I can help you with, or are you here to see Gabe?" Rick asked, and then he couldn't help adding, "What is that insanely delicious aroma?"

"Well, that's actually kind of the reason why I'm here," Angel confessed. She placed her hand on top of the old-fashioned wicker basket she'd set down on the desk closest to the door: Gabe's desk. There was an equally old-fashioned red-and-white-checkered cloth covering the length of the basket. It did nothing to suppress the warm aroma.

Gabe quickly crossed to her side. The conversation with Alma was still very fresh in his mind. Had someone tried to get in contact with her? Focusing strictly on her and not on the food that she'd obviously brought, it was hard to miss the concern in his voice.

"Is something wrong?" he asked.

The question caught her off guard. She looked at him quizzically. "No, why should it be?"

Alma stepped forward. "I think he's trying to say that it's the middle of the morning and he's wondering what you're doing here at this time."

Angel grinned at the man who so easily sent her pulse racing with just a touch. "I didn't know you came with subtitles," she said to him. "We were running late this morning," she reminded Gabe with a pleased smile.

Having alternated between making love and decorating the tree for half the night, they'd both slept through the alarm this morning and barely had time to get dressed before they were due at work. In the interest of time, breakfast had been a casualty.

"So I asked Miss Joan if I could bring you breakfast once the rush was over. Miss Joan said she'd only agree if I made enough for everyone in the office," Angel explained, pulling the checkered cloth from the basket. "So I did."

"I really do love that woman," Rick enthused, his mouth watering already.

"A word to the wise. Better not let Olivia hear you say that in that tone," Alma warned her boss with a laugh.

It was no secret that his attorney wife was out of her element in the kitchen. "When I met her, Olivia thought a stove was just an extra flat surface she could stack her legal papers on. I love her in a completely different way than I do Miss Joan," he explained even as he began to dig in.

Pleased, Angel finished unpacking everything she had brought to feed Gabe, the other deputies and the sheriff. Having arranged the different platters on the desk, she stood back to watch everyone dig in.

Conversations, laughter and a feeling of well-being permeated the office. Lingering and taking up the plates that Angel pressed into their hands, even Ben Walker and his wife seemed to be getting along.

Angel observed it all and smiled, contented. She'd never felt happier in her life. Deep down in her soul, she knew that for a fact, even if the life she was referencing only spanned three weeks.

She caught herself offering up a small prayer that nothing would ever change—even though she knew it probably had to.

But for now, everything was perfect and she was very, very grateful. And especially that she had Gabe.

Plate in hand, he sought her out and affectionately pressed a kiss to her temple. "You're the best," he told her just before he started eating.

*So are you,* she thought, deciding to tell him that when they were alone.

That made two things she needed to tell him when they were alone, she thought.

A smile of anticipation curved her mouth.

## Chapter Fourteen

Angel was still carrying on her silent debate the following late afternoon when she stopped by the sheriff's office again, this time with a filled-to-the-brim basket of her freshly fried chicken.

And then she finally decided, while watching Gabe polish off a second piece of the fried chicken, to wait with her news.

She wanted to pick just the right moment. The right moment to tell him she was pregnant.

She could hardly believe it herself. She'd gone to the town's only doctor, telling him that she just didn't feel "quite right." He'd suggested a full exam, just to rule out a few things. When he'd finished, he ran one final, simple test "just to be sure." And then he was. When he'd told her the results, that she was pregnant, she was stunned—and she couldn't stop smiling.

Ordinarily it might have been news that would have given her pause had Gabe not been Gabe. Had he been more like other men—men she had a feeling had crossed her path even though she couldn't summon anything concrete to back up her hunch—she would have been hesitant to mention this latest development because he might have viewed it as coming across like entrapment.

But Gabe had made it very clear to her that he cared about her, *really* cared about her. And besides, she wasn't going to attach any stipulations or requirements to her news. If there were steps to be taken after Gabe knew, well, they'd discuss it, both sides of it, later.

Angel was absolutely convinced that this was something good and perfect. Otherwise, why would she feel like singing constantly?

She'd even caught herself humming once or twice.

Like now.

And so had Gabe. He'd noticed the even more upbeat air than usual about her. Angel had been becoming steadily happier, he felt, but this wasn't just another small step in that direction. More like a giant leap.

"You look like the cat that swallowed the canary," he observed, reaching for yet a third piece of fried chicken. "Something up?"

She wanted to talk about this when they were alone and the setting was right. Much as she liked the people he worked with—as well as, she silently added, most of the town—she wanted this to be a private exchange between the two of them first. Then if he wanted to, they could shout it from the town square together. Or keep it their little secret a little while longer.

She was up for whatever he wanted to do.

"No, no canary," Angel replied. "Some chicken, maybe, but no canary." She looked around the office. Everyone was eating, but that could have been just because they were very hungry. "By the way, is it all right?

The chicken," she prompted, realizing that her question had sounded a little vague.

"All right?" Rick echoed with a grin as he dug into the container she'd brought. It was practically empty. "It's so far above 'all right' I don't think they've even invented a word for it yet." He paused as he took the first bite of the latest piece he'd just scored. "How did you learn how to cook like this?" he marveled.

Angel shook her head, a helpless, mystified expression on her face. "I have absolutely no idea," she admitted.

For a second, he'd forgotten that she still had amnesia. She'd become such a fixture in the town so quickly, it was easy at times to forget how she'd come to be here in the first place. "Right. Sorry," he apologized. "I didn't mean to—"

Angel wouldn't allow him to finish. She knew he hadn't meant to make her uncomfortable. If anything, everyone had gone out of their way to *make* her feel comfortable here, as if she belonged. As far as she was concerned, she belonged here far more than she did wherever it was that she came from.

"That's okay," she interrupted. "I know what you mean." She glanced at the swiftly depleting supply of food she'd brought. "Well, there was enough here for seconds and maybe thirds. If you want any more once that's empty, just give Miss Joan a call. I think there's still a little leftover at the diner."

Joe laughed softly, shaking his head. "Not if Harry's there," he commented, mentioning Miss Joan's husband. "The man really *loves* his fried chicken."

"Can't imagine *anyone* not loving this," Alma chimed it, indicating the all-but-denuded leg she was holding. "So, I take it that Miss Joan's hiring you to take Eduardo's place," she asked in between bites to polish off what was left of the piece—her third—she was holding.

To the surprise of all of them, Angel shook her head. "Actually, Eduardo changed his mind. He's decided to stay on a little longer."

Gabe had seen how happy she was, going to work at the diner every day. She really *enjoyed* cooking. This news had to have devastated her. "Well, he can't do that," he declared, feeling indignant for her.

"He can and he did. But it's all right," she assured Gabe, placing a calming hand on his arm, which no one in the office missed. "Miss Joan decided that since business has picked up so much lately, there's more than enough work for both of us."

She seemed oblivious to the little detail that she was the reason *why* it had picked up so much, Gabe thought.

She leaned forward now, as if sharing a secret even though she said it loud enough for all three deputies and the sheriff to hear. "She said having me there will keep Eduardo in his place."

Rick laughed. "I bet it will at that." Miss Joan, they all knew, was nothing if not extremely sharp in her dealings with the customers *and* her staff. Rick held up his latest finished piece as if it was exhibit "A." "This is really fantastic," he enthused. "Maybe you could give my wife some lessons."

"Olivia might take offense at you suggesting that she needs lessons," Alma pointed out tactfully.

Rick looked at her. "Olivia is the first one to admit that she can't cook."

Alma rolled her eyes, a pitying smile on her lips. "God but men are thick." She looked pointedly at her boss. "There's a big difference between her admitting it and you actually agreeing with her on that point."

"So agreeing with her is a bad thing?" Rick asked, confused.

"In this case, a very bad thing," Alma said. "You're supposed to tell her that you like her cooking."

It was Rick's turn to roll his eyes—and hold his stomach in mock agony. "I tell her that and she's liable to do more of it," he pointed out. The remark was followed by a shiver.

"Well, whatever you do, *don't* suggest she take cooking lessons," Alma advised.

Angel did her best not to laugh at the disappointed expression on Rick's face. Turning toward Gabe, she asked, "Are you about ready to go home?" She assumed he couldn't eat more than the four pieces he'd already consumed.

Wiping his fingers on the edge of his napkin, Gabe nodded. His shift was over and he just had to put something away. Rising from his chair, he told her, "Give me a couple of minutes and—"

Just then, the front door flew opened and a wild-eyed, maternal-looking woman rushed in. "I can't find Jason," Diane Lake cried without any preamble.

Dinner—what there was left of it—was instantly

forgotten as Rick rose to his feet and crossed to the woman. The latter looked as if she was on the verge of falling apart.

"It's going to be all right, Diane," Rick said gently, trying to calm her down. "When did you last see Jason?"

It took Diane a moment to remember. All her thoughts were apparently scattered. "A couple of hours ago. He came home from school and wanted to play in the back before supper was ready." There was fear in the woman's brown eyes as she turned them on Rick. "He's gone wandering off in the woods, I just know it. I told him not to—I always tell him not to—but he was mad at me…"

"Why was he mad?" Gabe asked. All three deputies had risen and closed ranks around the distraught woman, unconsciously forming a tight circle, as if the very act could somehow comfort her.

"I told him if he didn't get his grades up, we wouldn't get a Christmas tree this year." Her voice nearly broke. She struggled to continue. "That the one in the square would be enough." Tears were now sliding down her cheeks. She couldn't stop them. "I think he went to get one. Jason's just eight," she cried as if everyone in the room—except for Angel—didn't already know that fact. "He'll get lost."

"We'll find him," Rick promised firmly. He addressed each of his deputies. "I want you to spread out. Hit the diner, the Emporium, wherever you find more than just a couple of people. Round up every able-bodied man and woman you can get," he ordered. "We're going to comb those woods and get that boy back to his mother before daylight." He looked at the shaking woman. "It's going to be all right," he repeated firmly, willing her to believe nothing less. "Just hang in there."

"I'll come," Angel instantly volunteered as she pulled on Gabe's arm to get his attention.

Gabe flashed a smile at her. She didn't know the terrain the way they all did. It was incredibly easy to take a wrong turn and get lost—or fall off a cliff that's edge had been hidden by brush.

"Stay with Diane," he advised. "She's going to need someone."

Angel had a better idea. "I can take her to Miss Joan," she suggested. "That way, I can help search for the boy. Besides, Miss Joan's so much better than I am at this kind of thing."

Gabe really didn't want to say yes because he didn't want to risk her getting lost, as well. But he saw a stubborn expression enter Angel's eyes and knew it was useless to stand in her way. So, reluctantly, he agreed. "Okay, we'll take her to Miss Joan's together. I'll handle asking for volunteers at the diner," he told Rick, raising his voice to get the sheriff's attention.

Rick nodded, already hurrying out the door.

They left Jason's frantic mother in Miss Joan's capable hands.

"I've got just the tea for you," they heard the owner of the diner saying to Jason's mother. "It'll soothe your nerves. Kids are always running off," she said matter-of-factly, as if it was a fact of life that happened every day in Forever. "They'll have him back before you know it."

"When Miss Joan says it, it sounds like gospel," Gabe commented as he walked out of the diner right behind Angel.

Once outside, though, he forgot all about Miss Joan and looked at the only woman who had come to matter so very much to him. "Here are the rules. I want you around me at all times," he told her.

Under other circumstances, she would have readily agreed. Agreed and flirted a little, as well. But there was a small boy missing right now and every moment counted. And every moment they weren't out there, looking, was a moment lost and one less that Jason possibly have left.

"But shouldn't we spread out?" she asked. "We can cover more ground that way."

That simple fact was not enough for him to agree and let her go off on her own. He'd tie her up before allowing that to happen.

"In case you haven't noticed, it's already dark outside—and it's a lot easier to get lost in the dark. I'm not taking a chance on you disappearing like Jason. Now, if you give me an argument," he concluded seriously, "I'm sending you home."

She watched him for a long moment. He'd surprised her by sounding as stern as he did. Her reaction was also a surprise, because something inside of her rose up in semirebellion.

Angel's eyes met his. "And you actually think I'll stay there?" she asked him, amused.

Gabe sighed. The woman was getting bolder. And more stubborn. He supposed that was a good sign.

"Okay," he relented, "you can come—but you have to follow orders. There's got to be structure in the search." He wasn't going to be flexible about that. Under no circumstances was he going to allow her to go off on her own. He decided his best bet was just to level with her. "Look, I don't think I could stand it if you got lost out there somewhere, understood?"

Angel continued looking at him, but the rebellious feeling disappeared. Instead, another overwhelming feeling bubbled up within her like some awe-inspiring fountain. This had to be love. There was no other word for it and she'd been feeling it a lot lately.

After a beat, she nodded solemnly in response to his question.

"Understood," she echoed, then added a coda she figured he'd be okay with. "Two sets of eyes are better than one, right?"

Gabe laughed and nodded. "Right. Atta girl," he said with approval. "All right, we've got Mrs. Lake squared away with Miss Joan, let's get going."

She flashed him a smile. "Sounds like a plan to me."

"Yeah," he conceded. "Your plan."

And she damn well knew it, he thought. Not that he could fault her. Not for having feelings of empathy. She was just putting herself in Diane Lake's shoes and imagining what she would have felt if it was *her* little boy who'd gone missing.

SIX HOURS LATER, Rick decided to temporarily call off the search, at least until morning when they had more light—and more volunteers. He'd put a call into the county for bloodhounds and the dogs would be arriving with their handlers by seven.

Everyone could do with a few hours' rest.

"We can get started again at seven," he said over the two-way radio to his deputies and the other volunteers. Each group of searchers had been outfitted with the radio so they could stay in touch, and alert the others if they found Jason.

"Read you loud and clear, Sheriff," Gabe said over his own unit. Finished, he released the button that ended not only the exchange between Rick and the other groups, but the high-pitched squawking sound the unit was emitting, as well.

He didn't need to look at Angel to know that, although she was beat, she still wanted to continue. But pushing on, exhausted, wouldn't help.

Braced for an argument, he already began forming his rebuttal.

"A little rest might do us all some good, and besides—" He didn't get a chance to finish because Angel had her hand up and was motioning for him to be quiet. "Look, Angel, I know that you—"

"Shh!" Cocked her head a little more, straining to listen. "Don't you hear that?"

He listened—and heard nothing. "Hear what?" he pressed.

*"That,"* she emphasized impatiently. How could he not hear that? "Someone's crying." And with that, she hurried off in the direction of the crying she claimed to be hearing.

"I still don't—Angel, damn it," he cried, stunned to

see her take off like that after he'd strictly told her not to. "Don't go running off," he ordered, raising his voice so she could hear.

"Then follow me!" she shot over her shoulder. The next moment, she was picking up her pace, running in the general direction of the crying sound.

He was more worried than angry now. She didn't know this terrain, and not only could she get lost, but she could also wind up going over a ledge. Some paths ended abruptly out here.

Just like the one the day he first met her.

Remembering, his anxiety level tripled.

"Angel, you can't just—" Whatever else he was going to say was forgotten as, still chasing after her, Gabe thought he could make out the sound. "You're right. It *is* crying," he realized. They'd managed to locate Jason, even in the dark.

He slowed his pace just an iota in order to switch on the two-way radio. Calling Rick over the device, Gabe followed up his salutation by declaring with no small excitement, "I think we might have found him!"

Rick immediately ordered him to "Forward your position!"

Trying to keep Angel within his line of sight, Gabe rattled off his coordinates, estimating them as closely as possible. He looked down at the radio for a split second. When he looked up, Angel had disappeared.

There was an instant knot in his stomach, pulling so hard he couldn't breathe. "Damn it, I lost Angel!" was all he said before dropping his two-way radio and racing up ahead.

For a second, he'd abandoned all his training—and came precariously close to going over the ledge that had ended abruptly without warning. He caught himself just in time.

Four feet below where he stood right now was another, far more narrow ledge. And Angel was on it. Angel and the now-shaking, very frightened and cold little boy who was clinging to it.

"We've got you, Jason," Angel was saying to the boy. "It's going to be all right," she promised. She congratulated herself on sounding exceedingly calm, considering the fact that she'd just barely managed to hang on to this ledge when the other had suddenly stopped short and her misstep had sent her falling. Her heart still hadn't regained its regular beat. She'd come very close to getting killed, she realized.

But at least she'd found Jason.

"Who are you?" Jason asked, staring at her wide-eyed.

She mustered the biggest smile she could for his sake. "I'm Angel."

"A real angel?" he cried in wonder. "Does that mean I'm dead?"

"You're not dead," Gabe called out to the boy. "But she is a real angel." He glared down at her, knowing she couldn't make out his expression in this darkness. "Just one that doesn't listen very well." And one who almost gave him heart failure when he realized that she'd gone over the ledge, he added silently. Worst moment of his life *ever,* he emphasized.

"Told you I heard something" was all Angel said in her own defense.

The boy was shaking uncontrollably. Stripping off her jacket, she draped it around the boy's shoulders and closed the two sides around him to try to keep him warm.

"Don't move," Gabe ordered her, moving back from the ledge.

"Wasn't really planning on it," Angel called after him.

Gabe doubled back to fetch the two-way radio. He needed help. *Now.*

It took him a second to locate where he'd dropped it. His own hands were shaking—not from the cold but from the thought that Angel could have easily died tonight.

Damn it.

Pressing down on the communication button, he hailed Rick. "We're going to need a rope to pull the boy up from a ledge." He was getting ahead of himself, he realized. "Angel found Jason," he told Rick, feeling both proud of her and angry at the same time. Angry that she'd risked her life in order to get to the boy. One wrong move and he'd be putting in a call for a body bag.

He pushed the thought away, unable to handle it right now.

"Hang in there, Gabe, we're on our way," Rick told him.

"Hurry" was all he said before he made his way back to the edge of the ledge.

He wasn't taking any chances. He needed to keep

vigil, assuring himself that Angel was all right until they could get her and the boy back on ground that measured more than a foot across.

## Chapter Fifteen

The people in town were still talking about it the following day, how Forever's newest citizen had risked her life and saved Diane Lake's little boy, Jason.

If Angel believed otherwise, those thoughts were quickly dispelled when she walked into the diner with Gabe at eight the next morning. Rather than just drop her off, the way he'd taken to doing on his way to work, Gabe had decided to come in with her for a minute.

The customers seated at the counter and occupying the tables all turned around, almost in unison, and broke into a round of heartfelt, hearty applause.

Stunned, Angel looked around, fully expecting the applause to be meant for someone coming in behind her.

Except that there wasn't anyone behind her.

Flustered, she turned her head toward Gabe—away from the customers—and lowering her voice asked, "Why are they applauding?"

Gabe grinned, feeling so proud of her he could burst. "Because the only thing the people around here like better than a hero is a heroine," he said honestly. He saw the color rising in her cheeks and tried to eliminate her growing discomfort. "Hey, you earned this, Angel.

You risked your life—and damn near gave me a heart attack," he added, "getting that boy off the ledge. Now you get to take a bow."

"You might as well enjoy it, they're not about to stop," Miss Joan told her, coming around the counter and putting a protective arm around her. It was one of the few times that Angel could recall the woman smiling, let alone almost beaming at her. Her arm still around her shoulders, Miss Joan looked at the gathering. "Okay, settle down now. You're embarrassing her," she told the people in the diner, her eyes sweeping over each of them individually.

The applause died down—all except for one customer. He was sitting on a stool at the far end of the counter and turned around very slowly now to look knowingly in her direction. Tall, with chestnut-brown hair, the same color as his trim moustache, the man looked to be somewhere in his early forties.

No one recognized him.

He went on clapping, his hands meeting lowly, rhythmically.

"I said you're embarrassing her," Miss Joan repeated with emphasis as she glared at the stranger. She was not a woman who backed off, especially when met with opposition.

The man smirked at Miss Joan's statement. "Oh, she doesn't embarrass easily," he told Miss Joan, never taking his eyes off Angel. Except that he didn't call her that. He called her by another name. "Do you, Dorothy?" he asked.

Vacating his stool, the stranger moved like a panther stalking its prey and came over to where Angel was standing.

"Dorothy?" Gabe echoed.

He didn't like the looks of the man who sounded as if he was so familiar with Angel's life. Secretly, he'd been dreading something like this and now that it was happening, it was even worse than he'd imagined.

There'd been a small part of him all along that had whispered, *Some things are better left alone.* And now he had a gut feeling he knew why.

"That's her name. Dorothy Mandra," the stranger said, never taking his eyes off Angel. He moved even closer to her. "What's the matter, Dorothy? Not glad to see me?" he asked.

"She doesn't know you," Gabe cut in, coming to Angel's defense. He'd taken an instant dislike to this intruding stranger. "She has amnesia."

"Amnesia," the man repeated in a mocking tone. The smile that curved his lips was humorless and cold. "Pretty convenient."

"Look, mister—" Gabe began, physically turning the man away from Angel.

He could see that the stranger was crowding Angel. Even if she looked at him blankly as if she didn't know him, on some subconscious level, she had to have recognized him.

Her breathing had gotten slightly audible and definitely labored.

The man shrugged him off and then produced his ID. "That's 'Detective Mister,'" the stranger retorted glibly. Flipping open his wallet, his eyes narrowed slightly as he grew serious. "Detective Jake Wynters," he said, introducing himself. "With the San Antonio Police Department."

He added the latter for the sharp-featured older woman's benefit. She looked as if she could take him apart with her talons if he made any missteps.

Wynters doled his information out one piece at a time. "And Dorothy's my fiancée," he informed Gabe and the other customers. "My *missing* fiancée," he emphasized. "She went missing around the same time that my fifty-thousand-dollar bank account did." Smirking at her knowingly, he was all but on top of Angel as he uttered rhetorically, "Didn't you, Dorothy?"

Gabe felt as if someone had punched him straight in the gut. Still, he pulled Wynters back a second time even as Miss Joan put herself between the threatening detective and Angel.

"We didn't find any money on her," Gabe informed the outsider.

Wynters looked at the woman he'd come to bring back with him. "She's a bright girl. Dorothy would have hidden it somewhere so she could get to it later."

He was lying about the money, but in his experience, nothing turned people against one another more quickly than the hope of recovering hidden money. He wanted to make sure no one would try to get in his way and stop him from bringing her back with him. If they thought she was a thief, his job would be easier.

Miss Joan looked as unconvinced as Gabe felt. "You know him, honey?" she asked Angel.

She had to, Angel thought. Why else did she have

this sudden, overwhelming dread rising up within her? The very sound of his voice made her want to shrink back. And yet, she didn't recognize him, couldn't connect him to a single event in her life.

Couldn't remember *ever* having seen him.

She had no choice but to shake her head. "No, I don't know him," she said quietly.

Wynters snorted. "We had an argument just before she took off. She's just angry, that's all," he insisted, reaching for her.

Angel instinctively pulled back and now it was Gabe who stood between her and the San Antonio detective as Miss Joan protectively ushered her behind the counter and stood by her side. Miss Joan glared at Wynters.

"She says she doesn't know you," Gabe informed the stranger. "So maybe you should be getting on your way." It wasn't a suggestion.

Some of the other customers had risen from their seats, their stance silently adding weight to Gabe's words. For his part, the detective seemed totally unaffected.

"I thought she might try to pull something like this," Wynters said to Gabe as he took a manila envelope out of the inside of his jacket. Slipping out the contents, he held it in his hand. "Got pictures of the two of us, plus one of her in front of the restaurant where she used to work." He produced the latter, jabbing a finger at the background. "That's Slice of Heaven," he said for the benefit of the people who couldn't make out the restaurant's sign. And then he looked at Angel. "Bennett said to tell you that business hasn't been the same since you left. Your old job's waiting for you if you decide you want to come. To him," he added, the silent implication was that in *that* case she had a choice. As far as coming back to *him,* she only had one choice. To agree.

With equal skepticism and reluctance, Gabe forced himself to look at the photographs.

It was Angel all right.

His heart suddenly felt like lead in his chest.

"Satisfied?" Wynters asked, putting the photographs back into the envelope before returning the latter to his pocket. "Now, if you don't have any more objections, I'll be taking Dorothy home with me."

As the detective, who was a good four inches taller than Gabe, began to make his way around the counter in order to carry out his intent, Gabe grabbed hold of his shoulder and pulled him back for a third time, this time more roughly than before.

"No," Gabe said firmly.

"No?" the detective echoed incredulously. Any pretense at common courtesy totally evaporated. "Who the hell do you think you are, telling me no?" he demanded.

"Someone who's not going to let you just take Angel until she's ready to go." Gabe all but growled the words out.

Wynters gave him a once-over, a smug look entering his eyes. "What, she's your girlfriend now?" he taunted. "Her name's Dorothy," he insisted. "Not 'Angel.' And I'd be careful if I were you," he warned malevolently. "She'll play you with those big blue eyes of hers, then, when you're not looking, she'll make off with everything you've got except for the fillings in your teeth—

unless she's gotten handy with a pair of pliers since she took off."

He'd had about enough. "Like I said, I think you'd better leave, Detective," Gabe ordered.

The gloves were off. The expression on the detective's handsome face turned ugly. "The hell I will!"

The sound of a shotgun loudly being cocked caught everyone's attention.

The detective and Gabe both turned to look behind them. Eduardo had come out of the kitchen, the shotgun that Miss Joan kept in the back held poised in his hands. It was aimed directly at the stranger.

"You heard the deputy." Eduardo looked as if he'd welcome an excuse to fire. "Now go!"

"Put the shotgun down, Eduardo," Gabe ordered gruffly. He wasn't about to let the older man get into trouble because he'd been pushed too far by the taunting detective.

"I will, Deputy—as soon as this devil leaves Miss Joan's place," Eduardo answered. He was still aiming both barrels at Wynters, ready to discharge them at his target.

"He's leaving *now*."

The steely order came from the sheriff. Summoned by one of the customers on their cell phone, he'd come immediately. As he walked into the diner, there was an amiable look on his face, but one that meant business.

"Aren't you, Detective?" He added the title after glancing at the badge that Wynters was still holding in his hand. The man treated it like a magic talisman that would allow him to have access to everything.

"But I know this woman," Wynters insisted. "Isn't that why you sent out that poster with her picture on it? To have someone come and identify her? Well, I'm identifying her!" he concluded angrily, behaving as if he'd expected accolades, not road blocks.

"And we appreciate you coming all the way down to our little town, Detective," Rick said with barely veiled sarcasm. "But you can also appreciate the fact that I can't just send her off with someone she clearly doesn't remember." As if to back up his statement, Rick looked at the young woman in the center of this tug-of-war. "You don't remember him, do you?" he asked her, just to be sure.

"No." To assure herself, she shifted her eyes and glanced defiantly at the detective. "No, I don't," she told Rick honestly.

Wynters looked from her to the sheriff, stunned. "So that's it?" he demanded in disbelief. "You just take her at her word and I'm supposed to leave?"

"Not necessarily," Rick allowed. "We give Angel time to adjust," he said, no doubt deliberately using the name they'd given her, not the one that Wynters had used. "We give her time to remember. Until then, she stays here, in Forever."

Angry now, the detective was obviously trying to curb his temper. Rather than uttering the words that first raced to his lips, he bit them back and instead said, "I'll get my lawyer."

"Fine. And we'll get ours," Rick replied mildly. "By the way, my wife's a lawyer. She was formerly with the Norvil and Tyler law firm. You might have heard of them," Rick said, not above dropping the name of one of the most powerful and prestigious law firms in the western half of the country.

Judging by the look on the detective's face, he was familiar with the firm.

"Now, unless you have other business here…" he continued, his meaning very clear.

"He doesn't," Miss Joan informed the sheriff, making sure that the detective knew he was not about to be served in her establishment no matter what he might try to offer as payment.

"Then I'd suggest you leave your name and number with my office so we can reach you the moment Angel's memory comes back," Rick told the man pleasantly. "You'll find the office just north of here. It's right on your way out of town," he emphasized.

Muttering a string of curses audibly under his breath and threatening to return with enough legal power to mow down this "Godforsaken pimple of a nothing town," the detective stormed out of the diner.

Applause met his departure, adding insult to his gaping wounds.

Only when the diner door closed again did Angel release the breath she'd been holding all this time. Visibly relieved, she forced a smile to her lips.

Gabe looked at her. He could literally *feel* her fear, even if she tried to pretend she was fine. He remembered her first night in his house. She'd woken up, screaming because of a nightmare. Was this man the reason why? Had she dreamed about him coming after her? Was Wynters who she was running from?

His look was intense as he asked her, "Are you sure you don't remember him?"

Angel shook her head all the harder, as if in denial she hoped to make Wynters's very presence vanish from her mind.

"No. No," she repeated with feeling. "I don't know him."

Gabe nodded. He could see that she wanted to be done with this. At least he could do that for her. "Good enough for me," he told her.

"Angel, why don't you go home?" Miss Joan suggested, even as some of her customers met that suggestion with groans. They'd put up with a lot, all because they were all waiting for one of her breakfasts. "You've had a hell of a morning and maybe you should just—"

"No!" Angel refused with feeling. "I want to be here. I want to be doing something—cooking. It'll take my mind off that awful man with those flat eyes of his. Please?"

Her last words were all but drowned out by several of the customers, raising their voices to egg her on, enthusiastically backing her decision to stay and cook for them.

Faced with Angel's stubbornness and her customers growing demands to have Angel whip up her specialties, Miss Joan raised her hands in complete surrender.

"Hey, far be it for me to deny you something that makes you happy," she declared. "Besides, I think I'd probably have a mass rebellion on my hands if I didn't let you stay." She looked at the customers who were all but champing at the bit—threatening to *eat* that bit at any second if they weren't fed and fed soon. "Okay, boys, place your orders. She's staying," she declared.

A round of cheers met her words.

Touched, Angel smiled and retreated to the kitchen. Eduardo was waiting for her. "Thank you," she said simply, at a loss for any other words.

In threatening the detective with a shotgun unless he retreated, Eduardo had behaved as if he was her father, bent on protecting her. Something told her that had never happened to her before.

Whether that meant she had no father, or that she had a father who didn't care enough about her to come to her defense, she didn't know.

What she did know was that she liked the sensation of having someone watch over her.

*Like Gabe,* a small voice whispered.

Eduardo waved away her thanks. "I was not going to allow that man to take you away and leave me with all this cooking to do by myself," he grumbled. "Since you started to work here, I am not so overworked as I was before," he told her, refusing to give up the game altogether.

"Glad I can help," she told him, brushing a quick, grateful kiss against his grizzled cheek.

"Are you going to be all right here?" Gabe asked, sticking his head into the kitchen.

She waved away his concern. "I'll be fine, Gabe," she said with conviction. "I've got Eduardo, Miss Joan and, from the looks of it, a quarter of the town here to protect me." She grinned reassuringly at Gabe. She didn't want him to worry about her. "What could go wrong?"

The trouble was, he *knew* what could go wrong. There were a dozen things that could easily conspire against her. *More* than a dozen, he amended, glancing back over his shoulder at Angel.

But saying that to her would only make her worry again and the look that passed over her face when she first encountered the detective had slashed at his heart something fierce. He didn't want her experiencing that again if he could help it.

Gabe forced himself to walk out of the diner. He needed to get back to the sheriff's office. Specifically, he needed to get to a computer and find out exactly what there was to know about Detective Jake Wynters of the San Antonio Police Department.

He hoped it was a lot—and none of it good.

But either way, he wasn't about to let the man take Angel away with him, not even if her memory did come back to her.

He couldn't shake this sinking feeling that sending her off with Wynters would be tantamount to signing her death sentence. Someone had tampered with her brakes that first day she'd arrived and his gut told him it had been Wynters.

There was no way that man was going to come near her again. Not if he had anything to say about it, Gabe silently swore.

## Chapter Sixteen

She was being paranoid , but knowing that didn't help. Angel *still* couldn't shake the feeling that she was being watched even though, when she looked, no one was there.

That *detective* wasn't there.

For all intents and purposes, she was among friends and safe, she silently insisted.

She was at the diner, in the kitchen, going about her job with a healthy complement of people all around her, even in the kitchen. Eduardo seemed more alert—and vigilant—than she'd ever seen him and the waitresses were forever coming in to fetch *something*.

Even Miss Joan would find various pretexts that had her pushing open the swinging kitchen doors, looking for one thing or another.

Angel was on to all of them, knowing that everyone was just checking on her. Looking out for her. She more than appreciated it. Especially Miss Joan's efforts. The woman had to be peeking in at least every fifteen minutes if not more frequently.

Each time Miss Joan stuck her head in, Angel would flash a smile at the diner owner and continue to go about making whatever meal had just been ordered. As for Eduardo, it seemed as if he never really took his eyes off her even though the senior short-order cook went on working at a steady pace himself.

Angel pressed her lips together. She was surrounded by people who cared about her and she was protected. So why was this uneasy feeling rising up and taking hold of her over and over again, like the tide repeatedly lapping at the shore?

There was no logical reason to feel so edgy, she kept telling herself.

The problem was, she wasn't listening.

When it came time to leave, Angel breathed a sigh of relief, confident that she could finally get beyond this nagging uneasiness.

But that feeling was short lived.

Leaving the diner with Gabe, she could feel the hairs on the back of her neck rising up for no good reason. Nothing seemed to be out of place and that police detective who'd shown up this morning claiming to be her fiancé was nowhere to be seen.

Detective Jake Wynters had apparently disappeared after Rick had ushered him out.

Apparently.

Angel looked around her one final time before getting into Gabe's truck.

"He made you nervous, didn't he?" Gabe said rather than asked, sliding in behind the steering wheel.

She cleared her throat, buying herself some time, and then asked innocently, "Who?"

Gabe's smile was one of tolerance. "I think that's the

first time I've known you to lie." His smile deepened. "I'm happy to say you're not any good at it. You know who I'm talking about, Angel. That police detective who said you were his fiancée."

The very thought of a relationship with that detective made her shiver. She looked away from the man at her side and stared out the side window.

With a shrug she hoped looked disinterested enough, she said, "He seemed a bit intense, but he did go away."

Gabe had asked his sister to do some research on the man who claimed to be Angel's fiancé. The San Antonio police detective had an impeccable record with several commendations for bravery and a long list of accolades in his file according to what Alma had managed to dig up. He sounded like an honorable, upstanding law enforcement officer.

But Gabe couldn't shake the feeling that something was off. Either someone had deliberately cleaned up the man's file—or the detective was good at playing a dual role. Either way, Gabe had seen the fear in Angel's eyes when she looked at Wynters and that was enough to convince him that the detective wasn't going to get within ten feet of her.

"And I intend to see that he *stays* away," he told her, commenting on her conclusion.

*Oh, if only...*

Angel shook her head in response to his words. "You've got no reason to make him stay away, Gabe," she reminded him.

"I've got the best reason in the world," he contradicted. "You." Coming to one of the town's few traffic lights, he stopped, waiting for it to turn green again. He studied her profile thoughtfully as he waited. Her jaw was so rigid, it looked as if it could shatter. "You're sure you don't remember him?" he prodded gently.

Exasperated with herself, Angel shook her head. "I've tried over and over again, but I just can't pull up anything. I'm drawing a blank," she emphasized. Angel sighed, looking up at the vehicle's ceiling. "Wouldn't I be able to remember him if I actually *knew* him?"

While Alma had looked into Wynters's background, he'd spent the time trolling the internet, learning what he could about amnesia. The more he read, the less he seemed to know. Other than the condition defied boundaries.

"There are lots of different types of amnesia, Angel." It wasn't really an answer to her question, but it was the best that he could do.

"Right," she murmured. "And I've got the annoying kind." So where did that bring her? That she knew him? Or that she didn't?

"Maybe there's a reason you don't remember," Gabe suggested. "Maybe your mind is trying to protect you from something you couldn't deal with at the time and maybe still can't."

She rubbed her forehead. Her head was beginning to hurt. "Well, I won't know about that part until I remember, will I? *If* I remember," she amended, the frustration in her voice growing.

He tried to lighten the mood. "Right now, all you have to remember is that you've got a starving man with you."

And for that, she thought, she was eternally grateful. She was exceedingly lucky to have Gabe in her life and she knew it.

"Hungry, huh?" She laughed.

He glanced in her direction, his eyes sweeping over her. Loving what he saw. "In more ways than one," he assured her with feeling.

A warm feeling rushed over her, banishing everything else into the background, as she anticipated their evening together. All that mattered to her, *really* mattered to her, she reminded herself, was in this car with her, driving her to his home.

To *their* home, she told herself, taking tremendous solace in the feeling that generated.

Everything was going to be all right, she silently promised herself. Clinging to that promise. And when everything died down again, then she'd tell Gabe her news. That was another promise.

"NEED HELP?" GABE ASKED as she began to head to the kitchen the moment they walked into the house.

Angel shook her head. This was her domain and she did best in it alone. "Thanks for offering, but it would only take longer that way." She laughed.

Off the hook, he pulled his shirttails out of his trousers and began to unbutton his shirt. "Okay, then I'm going to go upstairs, wash up and change," he told her.

A nervous anticipation danced through him. It had been like this for most of the day. His uniform shirt hanging open, he shoved his hands into his pockets and did his best to appear as if he hadn't a care in the world.

Gabe curled his right hand around the item he'd tucked in there earlier. As his fingers made contact, his heart sped up, launching into double time.

He was still trying to decide whether to give it to her tonight, or tomorrow morning. Tomorrow was Christmas but the day was all but bursting at the seams with the activities planned into the framework of that special day. Alma and Cash had invited everyone in the family to come spend it at their house, and of course, there was the celebration in the town square.

But he wanted to snag a private moment with Angel because this was a private gift. He wanted it to be their secret for a few moments before they wound up sharing it with everyone else.

Tonight, after dinner. He'd give it to her after dinner, he decided, wavering again.

Moving toward the living room, Gabe caught sight of his reflection in the mirror. Angel was going to turn him down if he didn't do something about the way he looked, he thought. He looked one step removed from a saddle tramp.

"Right now, I wouldn't even say yes to me," he muttered under his breath. He needed to wash up—fast.

Whistling, he hurried up the stairs and into his bedroom to get a fresh set of clothes.

He didn't notice the shadow along the floor in front of him until it was too late.

ANGEL DID HER BEST to bank it down, but the tightness in her chest insisted on coming back the moment Gabe left her, quickly growing until it struck her as being almost too large to manage.

Certainly too large to ignore.

*Relax, you have to relax,* she silently ordered herself. *There's no reason to feel like a cornered rabbit. There's—*

Turning around, she barely stifled the scream that leaped to her throat.

"What are you doing here?" she demanded of the man who seemed to materialize out of nowhere. The very hair on her head began to tingle.

"Taking what's mine," Wynters snarled at her, abandoning any pretext of friendliness. Initially ready to forgive her when he'd arrived in town this morning, he was now furious with her for what she'd put him through. "Did you think you fooled me with that wide-eyed act of yours in the diner?" he demanded. Rolling his eyes and affecting a singsong voice, he mimicked what she'd said to the deputy this morning. "'No, I don't know him.' Like I was nobody," he snapped, reverting to his own voice. There was pure hatred in his dark eyes. "Well, it's not working. You know damn well who I am and you're coming with me, Dorothy."

He tried to grab her wrist in order to drag her away, but she pulled back. Fear clutched at her but she struggled to rise above it. "Don't call me that," she ordered, desperately trying to sound as if he wasn't really frightening her. "That's not my name."

"The hell it isn't," he spat out. "You're Dorothy, all right. Too bad your boyfriend had that poster circulated.

Up to that point, I really thought you were dead." His smile was cold, deadly.

Where was Gabe? What had he done with Gabe? Angel thought frantically.

"I guess I didn't do as good a job on those brakes as I thought. You've got a charmed life, Dorothy." He saw her looking toward the stairs. "Oh, your boyfriend?" he guessed, taking great pleasure in what he was about to say next. "Save your effort. He's not coming."

Fear for herself turned to anger and outrage, infusing her with strength. "What did you do to him?" she demanded.

He laughed contemptuously. "Don't worry, I didn't kill him. He's just going to have a killer headache when he wakes up. And an empty house. Now let's go!" Wynters ordered. This time, he produced a gun to back up his command.

She had no doubts that the man with the cold eyes could use the weapon on her without blinking. Still, she backed away until she felt the stove against her back. "He'll find you," she warned him defiantly. "He'll come looking for me and he'll find you."

"Doubtful." He taunted her. "That hayseed deputy'll be looking for a San Antonio detective and his slut—and we're not going back to San Antonio." He paused, letting his words sink in, savoring the fear he knew she had to be feeling. "I've got a whole new life planned for us. And if you don't do what I tell you, if you give me *any* trouble, you can be erased *real* quick," he promised malevolently.

"Now you either come with me, or I'm going to go

upstairs and finish your boyfriend off." He cocked the hammer on the weapon he had trained on her. The barrel was pointed at her throat. "You've got to the count of five to make up your mind. One, two, three—" He stiffened as he felt the cold steel against his neck.

"Put the gun down, Wynters," Gabe ground out. He'd barely come to and had to hold on to the walls as he made his way down the stairs, praying he wasn't too late. He didn't doubt for a second that the rogue detective was going to kill Angel, if not now, then soon. His type didn't tolerate being defied, especially not by a woman.

"Guess your head's harder than I thought," Wynters cracked. "The next time, I've gotta do it right." Then he spun around, head butting Gabe. The gun in Gabe's hand went flying.

With his vision blurred, Gabe scrambled to his feet, holding on to Wynters so the latter couldn't lunge at Angel.

The two men fought, winding up on the floor. Because his head felt as if it had been cracked open and was still spinning, Gabe suddenly found himself on his back. Wynters was on top of him, his hands wrapped around his throat. The detective had fifty pounds on him. Gabe struggled to claw his hands off, but he was rapidly losing consciousness.

From a great distance away, he heard it, heard the guttural scream as a crack of thunder echoed.

Or was that the sound of a gun being discharged?

He felt the pressure against his throat loosen. Beginning to suck in air, he still couldn't draw in enough to counteract the effects of being choked. His efforts to breathe were further impeded by the sudden heavy weight that slumped over him.

Wynters.

Angel dropped the gun she'd fired. Wynters's gun. She'd shot him with his own gun.

Everything seemed surreal.

Her legs felt like rubber as Angel pushed herself to run the short distance to where Gabe was lying on the floor. Shaking badly, she grabbed one of Wynters's arms and dragged his literally dead weight off Gabe. Once she'd separated the two, she dropped to her knees and anxiously scanned Gabe's body to see if he had any other wounds on him.

Why wasn't he opening his eyes? Her panic mounted. "Gabe, are you all right? Can you hear me?" She was sobbing now, afraid she'd been too late.

Behind her there was all sorts of commotion, but she could only focus on Gabe.

"Gabe, please. Answer me," she pleaded.

He opened his eyes then, just the barest hint of a smile feathering along his lips. "I was right. You really are something else," he told her weakly.

She let out a ragged sigh, sinking back on her heels. Tears fell freely. He was alive. Gabe was alive. She could handle anything else that came her way as long as Gabe was alive.

Only then did she realize people were talking to her, asking questions. It took her a few moments to orient herself and focus on what they were saying. And then she saw Rick. Angel could have cried with relief.

"Are you all right?" he asked her, taking her hands and helping her to her feet.

She slumped against him, completely spent. Only then did she answer his question. "Yes."

With one arm around her, supporting the young woman, he looked around Gabe's kitchen. A fight had obviously taken place before the gun was fired. Using a handkerchief, Alma was picking up the small handgun and depositing it into a self-sealing plastic bag.

"What the hell happened here?" he asked Angel.

But it was Joe who answered his question. "Looks like Angel shot an intruder." The deputy squatted down beside the body and put his fingers against the side of Wynters's neck.

She looked at the deputy, afraid to breathe. If Wynters was alive, he'd come after her. No matter how long it took, he'd find her.

"Is he—"

Thinking she was asking if the detective was alive, Joe slowly moved his head from side to side. "No, he's dead."

It was the tension and relief that brought on a fresh round of tears, not any sense of loss or grief. That had vanished a long time ago. Taking in a deep breath, she struggled to get hold of herself.

Beside her, Gabe had risen to his feet and now draped his arm across her shoulders, as much to comfort her as to help hold himself upright.

One look at her face and he knew. "You remember, don't you?"

The nod was all but imperceptible. Everything had

returned, not in bits and pieces, but almost in one blinding flash.

She recounted it very slowly, almost as if it had been a movie she'd been watching, starring someone else, not her.

"When I saw him choking you—when I thought he was going to kill you—it all came back, like it was there all along. Jake was a bully. He got off on terrorizing me. I knew he'd never let me go, that he would rather see me dead first. I knew I had to get away and I did. I got away clean. But then one day I accidentally found out that my mother had just died. She was the only family I had," she told him as tears gathered in her eyes. "I wanted to say goodbye.

"I waited until everyone left after the reception and I slipped into her house to get her album of pictures and her locket. My late father had given it to her and she told me that someday it was going to be mine," she explained.

"I was about to leave when I thought I heard a floorboard creak. I knew in my soul that it had to be Jake and I just took off without looking back." She sighed. "I guess I was right. He was the one who must have partially cut my brake lines." A look of disbelief washed over her face. "He'd told me more than once that if he couldn't have me, he'd rather see me dead than with another man."

She looked at Gabe, wanting him to know everything. "I never took his money. He lied about that. I wanted nothing to do with him. I just wanted to be free."

Gabe knew she wasn't the type to steal. "So your

name really is Dorothy Mandra?" he asked. It was going to take time for him to get used to that, he thought.

She shook her head. "No." That life was behind her and she wanted it to remain that way. "It's Angel." She looked up at Gabe, the man who had given her her name. The man who had given her her life. "My name is Angel," she repeated again with feeling.

"We're going to need a statement, Angel," Rick told her, deliberately using the name she'd chosen to stay with. "We'll take it the day after tomorrow," he added. "Tonight's Christmas Eve and tomorrow's Christmas, this will keep until after that."

But she shook her head. "No, I want to get this over with now, put it behind me once and for all."

"Your call," Rick told her obligingly. Turning toward one of the people who had been drawn by the sound of gunfire and had subsequently congregated around them, he said, "Get the doc out here."

"Then he *is* still alive?" she asked in horror, staring at Wynters's fallen body.

"No, he's dead all right." Rick's voice softened just a touch. "I want you and my deputy here checked out. Wouldn't want to risk losing either of you," he said matter-of-factly.

Gabe offered no resistance, just asked for an indulgence. "Can I have a minute, Sheriff?"

"You can have ten," Rick told him genially. "Just don't go wandering off."

"We'll be just over there," Gabe told him, pointing toward the pantry. Taking Angel by the hand, he went inside the pantry, switched on the overhead light and closed the door.

Most of the pantry shelves were empty. That still didn't explain what they were doing there. "Gabe?" she asked uncertainly.

"I've got something to say before this night gets any weirder," Gabe told her.

She braced herself, waiting to hear what she felt in her heart was going to be the beginning of the end. Their end. And why not? Taking up with her had almost cost Gabe his life. What man wanted a woman like that to keep hanging around?

"All right," she whispered, an unbelievable sadness clutching her heart. "Go ahead."

He reached into his pocket. Good, it was still there. He hadn't lost it in the fight.

"All right," he began, his mouth suddenly so dry it felt as if his tongue was going to stick to the roof of his mouth any second now, "before Doc starts poking and prodding me and Rick starts picking your brain apart for details about this horror show, I just wanted to ask you… I just wanted to ask you…"

This wasn't going to come out right, he thought. His head was really hurting him and all the words he'd rehearsed so carefully had temporarily vanished from his brain.

"Oh, hell," he muttered.

This was going to be worse than she thought. She could feel tears begin to sting her eyes. She decided to spare him the trouble. "That's all right, you don't have to say it," she told him.

Puzzled, he looked down into her upturned face. "I don't?"

"No." She pressed her lips together, afraid she was going to start sobbing. "I'll leave as soon as I give Rick my statement."

"Leave?" Gabe echoed. The pain he still felt around his neck was nothing in comparison to what his heart was suddenly going through. "Why would you leave?"

How could he ask her that? Was he playing some sort of a game?

Or was he?

"Because you want me to," Angel answered. "Don't you?"

"No, I don't," he cried with feeling. "What I want is to give you this," he said in an eruption of frustration, pulling out his hand and opening it to reveal an engagement ring lying in his palm. "I had a whole speech worked out, but now I can't seem to rem—"

Snatching the ring from him, Angle quickly slipped it on the proper finger on her left hand.

She didn't want a fancy proposal. All she wanted was him—for the rest of her life.

But first, she suddenly remembered her own news. "I have something I have to tell you first," she said, "before I give you my answer."

"What?" he asked uneasily.

She'd wanted to pick her time, but after what just happened, he needed to know—and the sooner, the better. "You're going to be a father."

He looked at her, stunned beyond words. "Are you saying—"

"I'm pregnant." And then she took a breath, knowing this could change everything. "So if you want to take your ring back—"

He didn't even hear her. His mind was stuck in first gear. "You're sure? You're sure you're pregnant?" he asked.

She nodded. "Very sure. But that doesn't mean you have to marry me."

"Yes, I do," he insisted. "I want my happy ending." He looked at her and said, "You still haven't given me your answer."

He was one in a million. And she loved him. "Yes," she cried, throwing her arms around his neck. "Yes, yes, yes," she repeated, uttering each word in between the kisses she rained on his face.

The final "yes" was followed by a long, soulful kiss that was equal parts joy and relief.

Which was the way Rick found them when, concerned by the silence, he finally opened the pantry door. Taking in the scene, the sheriff of Forever smiled knowingly and quietly closed the door again.

"I can always take the statement later," he murmured, pleased, as he walked away.

\* \* \* \* \*

# REQUEST YOUR FREE BOOKS!
## 2 FREE NOVELS PLUS 2 FREE GIFTS!

## LOVE, HOME & HAPPINESS

**YES!** Please send me 2 FREE Harlequin® American Romance® novels and my 2 FREE gifts (gifts are worth about $10). After receiving them, if I don't wish to receive any more books, I can return the shipping statement marked "cancel." If I don't cancel, I will receive 4 brand-new novels every month and be billed just $4.49 per book in the U.S. or $5.24 per book in Canada. That's a saving of at least 14% off the cover price! It's quite a bargain! Shipping and handling is just 50¢ per book in the U.S. and 75¢ per book in Canada.* I understand that accepting the 2 free books and gifts places me under no obligation to buy anything. I can always return a shipment and cancel at any time. Even if I never buy another book, the two free books and gifts are mine to keep forever.

154/354 HDN FEP2

Name _____ (PLEASE PRINT)

Address _____ Apt. #

City _____ State/Prov. _____ Zip/Postal Code

Signature (if under 18, a parent or guardian must sign)

### Mail to the **Reader Service:**
**IN U.S.A.:** P.O. Box 1867, Buffalo, NY 14240-1867
**IN CANADA:** P.O. Box 609, Fort Erie, Ontario L2A 5X3

Not valid for current subscribers to Harlequin American Romance books.

**Want to try two free books from another line?**
**Call 1-800-873-8635 or visit www.ReaderService.com.**

\* Terms and prices subject to change without notice. Prices do not include applicable taxes. Sales tax applicable in N.Y. Canadian residents will be charged applicable taxes. Offer not valid in Quebec. This offer is limited to one order per household. All orders subject to credit approval. Credit or debit balances in a customer's account(s) may be offset by any other outstanding balance owed by or to the customer. Please allow 4 to 6 weeks for delivery. Offer available while quantities last.

**Your Privacy**—The Reader Service is committed to protecting your privacy. Our Privacy Policy is available online at www.ReaderService.com or upon request from the Reader Service.

We make a portion of our mailing list available to reputable third parties that offer products we believe may interest you. If you prefer that we not exchange your name with third parties, or if you wish to clarify or modify your communication preferences, please visit us at www.ReaderService.com/consumerschoice or write to us at Reader Service Preference Service, P.O. Box 9062, Buffalo, NY 14269. Include your complete name and address.

HARI1B

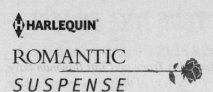

# HARLEQUIN®

## ROMANTIC
## SUSPENSE

**Get your heart racing this holiday season with double the pulse-pounding action.**

# *Christmas Confidential*

### Featuring

### *Holiday Protector* by **Marilyn Pappano**

Miri Duncan doesn't care that it's almost Christmas. She's got bigger worries on her mind. But surviving the trip to Georgia from Texas is going to be her biggest challenge. Days in a car with the man who broke her heart and helped send her to prison—private investigator Dean Montgomery.

### *A Chance Reunion* by **Linda Conrad**

When the husband Elana Novak left behind five years ago shows up in her new California home she knows danger is coming her way. To protect the man she is quickly falling for Elana must convince private investigator Gage Chance that she is a different person. But Gage isn't about to let her walk away…even with the bad guys right on their heels.

**Available December 2012 wherever books are sold!**

www.Harlequin.com

HRS27801

*The Bowman siblings have avoided Christmas ever since a family tragedy took the lives of their parents during the holiday years ago. But twins Trace and Taft Bowman have gotten past their grief, courtesy of the new women in their lives. Is it sister Caidy's turn to find love—perhaps with the new veterinarian in town?*

*Read on for an excerpt from*
*A COLD CREEK NOEL by* USA TODAY
*bestselling author RaeAnne Thayne, next in her ongoing series* THE COWBOYS OF COLD CREEK

\*\*\*

"For what it's worth, I think the guys around here are crazy. Even if you did grow up with them."

He might have left things at that, safe and uncomplicated, except his eyes suddenly shifted to her mouth and he didn't miss the flare of heat in her gaze. He swore under his breath, already regretting what he seemed to have no power to resist, and then he reached for her.

As his mouth settled over hers, warm and firm and tasting of cocoa, Caidy couldn't quite believe this was happening.

She was being kissed by the sexy new veterinarian, just a day after thinking him rude and abrasive. For a long moment she was shocked into immobility, then heat began to seep through her frozen stupor. Oh. Oh, yes!

How long had it been since she had enjoyed a kiss and wanted more? She was astounded to realize she couldn't really remember. As his lips played over hers, she shifted her neck slightly for a better angle. Her insides seemed to give a collective shiver. Mmm. This was exactly what two people ought to be doing at 3:00 a.m. on a cold December day.

He made a low sound in his throat that danced down her spine, and she felt the hard strength of his arms slide around her, pulling her closer. In this moment, nothing else seemed to matter but Ben Caldwell and the wondrous sensations fluttering through her.

Still, this was crazy. Some tiny voice of self-preservation seemed to whisper through her. What was she doing? She had no business kissing someone she barely knew and wasn't even sure she liked yet.

Though it took every last ounce of strength, she managed to slide away from all that delicious heat and move a few inches away from him, trying desperately to catch her breath.

The distance she created between them seemed to drag Ben back to his senses. He stared at her, his eyes looking as dazed as she felt. "That was wrong. I don't know what I was thinking. Your dog is a patient and…I shouldn't have…"

She might have been offended by the dismay in his voice if not for the arousal in his eyes. But his hair was a little rumpled and he had the evening shadow of a beard and all she could think was *yum*.

\*\*\*

*Can Caidy and Ben put their collective pasts behind them and find a brilliant future together?*

*Find out in A COLD CREEK NOEL, coming in December 2012 from Harlequin Special Edition. And coming in 2013, also from Harlequin Special Edition, look for Ridge's story….*